"Oh, it's

The fragran ght air, and the hillside made her rea ey were.

"It is, isn't it? Not near as lovely as you, though," Nate said.

Meagan caught her breath at his words. She wasn't sure what to say, except, "Thank you."

Following a lull in the music, the orchestra began to play again, and Nate turned to her. "A waltz. Perfect. Won't you let me show you some steps now?"

"I—yes, please," Meagan said. How thoughtful of him to get her away from any chance of ridicule for her clumsiness.

He bowed and slipped his right arm around her waist, holding out his left hand for hers. Meagan slipped her hand into his, and he drew her nearer. "One, two, three," Nate began to count as he showed her the steps. "One, two, three." The pressure from his hand told her when to turn. "One, two, three. You're getting it. One, two, three."

Meagan found it quite easy to follow his lead, the slight pressure on her back telling her when and in what direction he wanted her to turn. She lost track of time and was quite disappointed when the music ended. Nate sighed and kept his arm around her for a moment before letting her go. "You are an excellent student. Would you like to go in and dance around the ballroom floor now?"

"Oh. . .I'm not sure I'm ready for that—to dance in front of everyone. But thank you for the lesson. I enjoyed—"

"Another waltz," Nate interrupted as the music began again. "Let me have one more dance out here, then." He looked down into her eyes and smiled. Reaching out and tucking an errant curl behind her ear, he whispered, "Please."

He was asking her to do the very thing she wanted—to step into his arms again. "All right."

JANET LEE BARTON and her husband, Dan, have recently moved to Oklahoma and feel blessed to have at least one daughter and her family living nearby. Janet loves being able to share her faith and love of the Lord through her writing. She's very happy that the kind of romances the Lord has called her to write can be read by and shared with women of all ages.

Books by Janet Lee Barton

HEARTSONG PRESENTS
HP434—Family Circle
HP532—A Promise Made
HP562—Family Ties
HP623—A Place Called Home
HP644—Making Amends
HP689—Unforgettable
HP710—To Love Again
HP730—With Open Arms
HP745—Family Reunion
HP759—Stirring Up Romance

Don't miss out on any of our super romances. Write to us at the following address for information on our newest releases and club information.

Heartsong Presents Readers' Service
PO Box 721
Uhrichsville, OH 44683

Or visit www.heartsongpresents.com

A Love for Keeps

Janet Lee Barton

Heartsong Presents

To my Lord and Savior, for showing me the way. To Dan, who has encouraged me from the beginning; Nicole, who reads even when she doesn't always feel like it; and Mariah and Paige, who give me a wealth of ideas.

I love you all—with all my heart.

A note from the Author:
I love to hear from my readers! You may correspond with me by writing:

Janet Lee Barton
Author Relations
PO Box 721
Uhrichsville, OH 44683

ISBN 978-1-60260-287-8

A LOVE FOR KEEPS

Our mission is to publish and distribute inspirational products offering exceptional value and biblical encouragement to the masses.

PRINTED IN THE U.S.A.

one

Meagan Snow walked out of the bank, trying not to let her mother know how discouraged she felt. All she had to do was look at the older woman to see she felt the very same way, if not more so.

"Meagan, I don't know why I let you talk me into doing this," Elsie Snow said as they walked down Main Street to the third bank they would try that morning. "We've already been turned down by two different banks. We should probably just go on home."

"Mama, I am not giving up until we have no choice." She couldn't. It had been one thing for her mother to take in wash to help ends meet since Papa died. Meagan and her sisters, Becca and Sarah, could help her with that. However, the fact that Mama felt she had to take a part-time job helping to get the newly built Crescent Hotel ready to open was more than Meagan could take. It was time, as the oldest daughter, to help more than she had been. The mending she took in wasn't enough. God had blessed her with a talent, and she intended to put it to use to help provide for her family. She could do no less. If they were successful in getting a loan, her mother would be able to quit the hotel position before long.

They entered the Connors Bank and walked up to the receptionist. "Good morning. I'm Meagan Snow and this is my mother, Elsie. We'd like to see a loan officer, if possible," she said.

The receptionist gave Meagan and then her mother an appraising look before answering, "I'll see if Mr. Brooks has time to see you. Please take a seat right over there." She pointed to several settees in what Meagan assumed was a waiting area.

"Thank you," Meagan's mother said. One settee had a cuspidor sitting to the side of it. Meagan and her mother chose the other one. The way Mama twisted her lace-trimmed hankie between her fingers told Meagan how nervous she was.

Meagan covered those fingers with her hand and squeezed. "It's going to be all right, Mama. This bank is much bigger than the others are. It surely has more money to loan." She tried to sound positive, but the truth was she didn't know what they were going to do if they couldn't get a loan from this bank.

"I don't think it's that the other bankers didn't have the money, dear. I'm sure they think we are a bad risk. Moreover, I'm afraid this one isn't likely to be any different. The look on the impertinent young woman's face tells me that."

"Yes, I know. However, we know that we are not bad risks! And I will do my best to convince the bank manager of just that."

It seemed they waited for a long time, but it was really only a few minutes. A nice-looking man followed the receptionist out of a nearby office, and as she pointed in their direction, he nodded and headed their way. He didn't seem at all like the other two men they'd met with that day. Those men had been much older and. . .*stuffy* was the word that came to mind. The younger man who was striding over to them was of medium height, broad shouldered, and had deep brown hair. When he reached them, Meagan observed that his brown eyes had flecks of gold in them, and he was quite handsome when he smiled and held out his hand to her mother.

"Good morning, ladies. Mrs. Snow, Miss Snow, I'm Nate Brooks. What can I do for you today?"

"We need to apply for a business loan," Meagan stated, bringing his attention to her.

"I see." He paused and looked from Meagan to her mother and back again. "And what kind of loan are you looking to procure?"

"My daughter is a wonderful seamstress. She would like to start a dressmaking business in our home."

"Oh, I see." He nodded and motioned for them to follow him. "Please, come into my office and we'll see what we can do."

Meagan was afraid to get her hopes up, but this was the first time they had been invited inside an office and the first time anyone had seemed willing to listen to them. She prayed silently. *Dear Lord, please let this man see that we can make this business work. Please let him sense that we honor our word and will pay back every penny we borrow. Please let him lend us what we need, Father.*

Her opinion of the banker raised another notch when he held out a chair for her mother. She started to pull out her own chair, but his hand brushed hers as he did it for her. Meagan wasn't prepared for the way her pulse began to race at the slight touch. She took the seat and tried to compose herself. This was a business meeting, after all.

❧

Nate had held his office door open for the women, and once they were inside, he pulled out chairs, first for Mrs. Snow and then for her daughter, who'd started to pull out her own.

He wasn't sure if he could help them at all, but he hadn't been able to turn them away. The expression on the older woman's face was one of gracious resignation, and his heart had gone out to her. The daughter had more of a look of determination, and he was curious to hear what she had to say. She was lovely with black hair worn up in the style of the day. He wasn't sure what they called it, but nearly every young woman he knew wore theirs dressed similarly. The style was very flattering to Miss Meagan Snow. She was quite striking with her big blue eyes and long dark lashes, and she'd smelled good when he pulled out the chair for her. . .of lavender water or some such thing. Nate brought his thoughts up short. He needed to keep his mind on business. "Please, tell me a little about yourself," he said to the older woman.

"Well, I am a widow. My husband passed away a couple of years ago. He worked for the railroad. Then he came down with rheumatism, and for a while, it looked as if he was going to get better. But even the springs couldn't help him. He came down with the influenza and never recovered."

"I'm so sorry." That explained why these two women needed a source of income.

"Thank you. He did provide a house for us, free and clear, but we need income and we're willing to put our home up as collateral."

He glanced at the younger woman and saw that she was watching her mother closely. It was obvious that she felt protective of her. He focused his gaze on Mrs. Snow, also. "You say you want to start a dressmaking business in your home?"

"Yes, we do. Well, it will be my daughter's business. She's the dressmaker. And a better one I've never seen. She's even designed a few of her own."

"Is that right, Miss Snow?"

"Yes. My mother has taken a *temporary* position at the Crescent. But I feel it is my duty, as the oldest child, to help bring in an income, and I believe I can make this work." Her blue gaze met his from across the desk. "I don't want Mama working outside the home any longer than necessary, and I'd never agree to us putting our home up to secure the loan if I didn't believe I could make the shop a success."

"Have you had any formal training?"

"No, Mr. Brooks, I have not. But I learned the basics from my mother—"

"She's gone well past the basics," Meagan's mother interrupted. "She's being much too modest. She's expanded her knowledge well past mine by keeping up with the styles and making clothes for the whole family—I have two other daughters. And she's even been paid to make frocks for some of our neighbors and friends."

"I see." He looked at Miss Snow. "So this will be your business?"

"Yes, sir. It will be."

"And what is it you need to set this dressmaking shop up?"

"Well, we would need to turn one of our parlors into the actual shop or add on to our home." Miss Snow took a folded sheet of paper out of her reticule and handed it to him as she continued, "I'd need a new sewing machine and enough fabrics and trims to be able to offer my clients good choices."

He glanced at the paper. That she'd looked into what it would take to open her own shop was very apparent as he asked more questions.

"What kind of frocks do you specialize in?"

"I can make anything from everyday frocks to ball gowns." She seemed quite confident of her capabilities, and Nate wanted to give them a chance. "I think that your idea may be a good one. Still, before I could commit to lending you the money you need, I would want to visit your home and see what would be involved in turning part of it into a shop. And"—he looked at Miss Snow—"I'd need to see some samples of your work."

He wasn't sure if she would raise any objections but didn't see how she could.

"That would be fine," she said. "When would you like to come to our home?"

He looked at his schedule. "Would tomorrow at three o'clock be all right?"

"Will that be all right with you, Mama?" the daughter asked.

"I'll be home from the Crescent by then. Three will be just fine," the mother replied.

"Good." Nate stood, signaling the end of the meeting. The two ladies did the same. "I'll see you tomorrow at three, then."

He showed them out of the office, and as they thanked him and walked away, they looked so very happy that he hoped he didn't have to disappoint them.

☙

Meagan felt almost giddy when they walked out of the bank and started for home. "Oh, Mama, I think he's going to loan us the money!"

Her mother's smile told her she was every bit as hopeful as Meagan was. "I hope so, dear. He has kind eyes, and he certainly listened to us. He could have told us no today, so he must seriously be contemplating making us a loan."

"I'm sure he is." Meagan silently prayed that Nate Brooks was as good a man as he appeared to be and that he would approve the loan. Otherwise, she wasn't sure what they were going to do. But she knew that God would provide a way for them to get by. He always had.

It was amazing how much brighter the mid-February day seemed as they branched off Main at Spring, continuing past some of the homes that were built on the rocks above. Most of the houses had wide porches overlooking the road below. Meagan loved the way Eureka Springs was built on winding roads up and down the mountainsides. They continued on Spring, up the hill to Mountain, and then to the corner of Mountain and Montgomery, where they lived. The air seemed a touch warmer and the sky bluer than when they'd first started out. The pine trees even seemed greener. It wouldn't be long until winter gave way to spring, and Meagan could feel the change beginning. She'd been so concerned with the business of the day and worries about her family that she hadn't taken time to enjoy the beautiful day.

Her sisters must have been watching for them because as soon as Meagan and her mother rounded the corner, the girls ran out of the house to meet them.

"Well," ten-year-old Becca said, "did you get a loan?"

"And is Mama going to get to quit working so hard?" fifteen-year-old Sarah asked.

"We're hoping so," Meagan said. "Mr. Brooks will be coming tomorrow to look at the house and see how we mean to turn part of it into a shop. And he wants to see samples of my work."

"And then we'll get the loan?" Sarah asked.

Mama put an arm around her as they walked up the steps to the front porch and inside the house. "We hope so. But we want to make sure the house is as clean as it can be and that there aren't any stains on the dresses Meagan has made us."

"Mama, our home is always clean," Sarah said.

"I know. But we want it spotless for tomorrow." Of one accord, they headed to the kitchen, where they always discussed important things.

"We'll help, Mama," Becca said.

"I know you will, dear," their mother said, putting on the teakettle. "Let's have a bite to eat, and then we will get busy."

"What are we going to do if he says no?" Becca asked. "Before long, I'll be able to work at the Crescent, too."

"Maybe I can help clean Mrs. Elliot's house," Sarah added. "She's gettin' old and—"

"Girls, you aren't going to have to go to work. If Mr. Brooks says no, I'll keep working at the Crescent Hotel. It's not bad, really."

"And I can still sew for people. I just won't be able to charge as much."

"Everything is going to be all right, girls. I'm sure Mr. Brooks is going to loan us some money. We just have to make the best impression we can." Mama let out a big sigh and smiled. "But let us pray about it." She bowed her head, and her daughters did the same. "Dear Father, You know what we want and need. You've given Meagan a wonderful talent, and she wishes to use it to help this family. We pray that, if it's in Your will, we will get the loan we need to get Meagan started in her dressmaking business. But we only want it if it be Your will. It is in Jesus' name we pray. Amen."

"Amen," Meagan and her sisters said in unison.

"It's time to get to it," Mama said. "I'm so thankful I don't have to go into work today. We have much to do."

Meagan put on an apron and began cutting thick slices of bread to go with the soup her mother had put on before they left the house that morning. They enjoyed their meal but didn't dawdle over it. They had a lot to get done in a short amount of time.

Sarah was right. Their home was always clean. Still, so much counted on Nate Brooks's impression of it and them, that they did a thorough cleaning much like what they'd done just a few weeks ago. The good thing was that they *had* cleaned so well then. While Meagan took the rugs outside and beat them until there was no dust left to fly, Mama went over to Mrs. Morrison's to ask if Meagan might be able to borrow the dresses she'd made her so that she could show them to Mr. Brooks the next day. Becca mopped floors, while Sarah dusted every inch of the house.

By the time their mother returned from Mrs. Morrison's, they were ready for a break. Meagan brewed a pot of tea while her mother told her about the visit. "Nelda said she would run the dresses over in the morning. She wants to make sure they are pressed. She is so excited for you, dear."

"Mama, we don't even know if we'll get the loan. It's a little premature for her to be excited."

"She's sure we will get the loan and even offered to come tell Mr. Brooks how much she loves your creations, if we need her to."

"That's very sweet of her. I hope he'll be able to tell the quality of my work by looking at it himself. But it's nice to know that Mrs. Morrison will give me a good recommendation, if we need it." Meagan smiled and took a sip of tea.

"If we had more time, we could go all over town collecting what you'd made. You'd have more frocks to show him."

"It will be fine, Mama. We have a lot to show him. And I have some of my designs I can bring out, too."

"He's going to love them all," Sarah assured her. "Why, we

look as good as anyone else at school or at church."

"Thank you, Sarah." Meagan gave her younger sister a hug. "I'm very hopeful all will go well."

They finished their tea and then pitched in to shine the windows. By early evening, they were all ready to stop for the day as they heated up the soup left over from their noon meal.

"The house fairly shines, it's so clean," Becca said.

"Yes, it does. Mr. Brooks will find no dust in this house tomorrow," Meagan said. "Now all that is left to do is to look over the clothing and make sure it looks fresh and clean. I'll do any mending needed tonight before I go to bed."

"I don't think there will be much mending—you always keep up with that so well," Mama stated. "But we'll check, just to make sure, and I'll brush whatever needs only that. Tomorrow we can take turns pressing."

"Thank you, Mama." Meagan sent up a silent prayer. *Dear Father, thank You for Mama. Please help us to get this loan so that she doesn't have to work so hard. You know what we need, Lord. I trust that You will provide.*

Meagan sighed as she headed upstairs to see what needed mending. So much depended on the outcome of Mr. Brooks's visit. It had been so hard to lose Papa. And then to see her mother so willingly give up the household help they'd had ever since Meagan could remember. . .well, that was hard to watch. Meagan didn't mind helping her mother at all. What she did hate was the way some of her mother's friends had just quit calling on her or had stopped sending her invitations. To make things worse, her mother felt it necessary to get a job at the hotel.

Meagan had been trying to help, taking in mending for neighbors and sewing for them. But she didn't charge much because she felt they were doing her a favor by hiring her. She could make more money for the family, but she would have to go into business to do so. Their future hinged on tomorrow's meeting.

two

Nate wouldn't have gone to Abigail's that evening except that she made it so very hard for him to say no. She was his late wife's sister and the aunt of his six-year-old daughter. They were family, and she never failed to remind him of it. Not to mention that she was the daughter of the owner of the bank Nate managed. Mr. Connors had made no secret that his daughter knew many rich people who were always in need of a banker. To Jacob Connors's way of thinking, Nate needed to mingle and make friends of them all.

Abigail always wanted Nate there for a number of reasons. For one thing, she needed his support at these social functions, and his presence was a way to help the bank's business, too. After all, she invited people who were Nate's clients—or certainly should be. Of course, she was a banker's daughter and thought along the same lines as her father—or so she said.

Nate sighed as he raised the knocker on her front door. Abigail had moved into her own home several years before when she'd inherited it from her grandmother. It wasn't a large home, but it was very nice and in one of the well-to-do neighborhoods in Eureka Springs.

Normally, she hired a butler for her parties, but tonight she opened the door herself and greeted him with a kiss on the cheek, as she always did. It never failed to make him uncomfortable. He had a feeling that she would like him to make it a real kiss, but she was Rose's sister and he just couldn't do that. He had no doubts that if he asked Rose to marry him, she'd have them walking down the aisle in a matter of weeks. He wasn't ready for that step.

"I'm so glad you came, Nate. Thank you for arriving early."

"You say that every time, Abigail."

"I mean it every time." She smiled and batted her eyelashes at him as she took hold of his arm and led him into her large parlor. "How is my Natalie tonight?"

"She wanted to come, too. I told her it was one of your stuffy adult parties and she wouldn't enjoy herself."

"Nate!"

"Well, she wouldn't. And she agreed. I promised her I wouldn't be late."

"You always manage to leave early, Nate."

"I have a daughter to take care of, Abigail."

"I know that. You could have brought her over and put her to bed here."

"We've been over that before, Abigail." Occasionally, he had let Natalie stay overnight with her aunt Abigail, but that was only when he felt Abigail could give her the attention she needed.

"I know. I'll have just the two of you over for dinner later in the week."

"I'll tell her."

Nate was relieved when a knock at the door announced her other guests were beginning to arrive. He became weary of one-on-one conversation with Abigail after a few minutes. He greeted the others and mingled as much as he could before they were called to dinner. Two of her best friends, Jillian Burton and Rebecca Dobson, had come with their current suitors. Nate knew them through banking, too. Jillian's beau was Reginald Fitzgerald, who ran his family's jewelry store. Rebecca's current beau was Edward Mitchell, who'd just opened a new furniture store in town.

Several other couples whom he'd only met a time or two showed up, but he was certain that if they were anyone he needed to know better, Abigail would see that he did. For now, he just wanted to eat and get home to his daughter. Abigail employed a housekeeper and hired an extra cook for her parties. When the housekeeper let Abigail know that dinner was ready to be served, Nate was glad. He would get home that much sooner.

The help served several courses that included roast duck and creamed potatoes with tiny English peas and crusty rolls. The food was wonderful, and Nate was able to enjoy it as he only needed to give half an ear to Abigail and her friends discussing the upcoming spring social season in Eureka Springs. The ladies' talk about ball gowns and dressmakers, however, caught his attention and held it.

"I don't know what we are going to do with Miss Elliot marrying and moving away at the end of the year," Jillian said.

"We must get orders in quickly if we are to have the newest styles for this season," Rebecca added.

"This town could use several more dressmakers. I don't want to have to start going away to get my frocks," Abigail said, "but I don't know that we'll have much choice if we keep losing seamstresses."

Nate didn't say anything, but if Miss Meagan Snow was as good a dressmaker as her mother claimed, setting them up in business might prove to be a good risk—a very good one, indeed.

❧

Meagan woke on Tuesday, feeling both excited and apprehensive. She and her mother had worked into the night, too wound up to sleep, but they had only a few frocks to press.

They felt confident that Mr. Brooks would appreciate their efforts.

As she pulled on a wrapper and hurried downstairs to finish the pressing before getting dressed, Meagan took a deep breath and tried to appear calm. She didn't want her mother or the girls to see how nervous she was. That would only make them apprehensive. Besides, she'd prayed and put it all in the Lord's hands, and He would take care of it. They'd cleaned the house until it sparkled, and she was making certain that she would be showing Mr. Brooks her best work. There wasn't anything else she could do except wait on his decision.

"Good morning, dear. Mrs. Morrison brought over the morning dress and the dinner dress you made her. She made sure they were clean and pressed. She said if we need her to come meet Mr. Brooks to let her know. She'll be glad to."

"That's very nice of her." Meagan looked over the two dresses: the dinner dress, a crimson- and cream-striped sateen; and the morning dress, a blue- and green-checked gingham. "She has taken very good care of them. They look like they did the day I finished them."

She carefully laid them in her room until time to bring them out to show Mr. Brooks. While her mother made breakfast for the younger girls, she finished the pressing. Then her mother went to work, the girls went to school, and Meagan spent the rest of the morning laying out everything she planned to show Mr. Brooks. She loved the last housedress she'd made for Becca. It was of patterned blue and white batiste with three rows of pleated ruffles at the hem, the neckline, and wrists, and a skirt that draped gracefully in the back. Meagan was happy with the way her mother's new brown brocade visiting dress had turned out, too, with its side drape, trimmed in gold. She looked lovely in it.

After making sure everything looked as good as it could, Meagan put on her favorite afternoon dress. It was brown, cream, and blue plaid gingham, with a front drape. She went down to the kitchen to heat up her curling irons and put her hair up, curling a few tendrils around her face. Finally, there was nothing more to do but wait until Mr. Brooks arrived. . . except to pray that he would decide to approve their loan.

※

Mr. Brooks arrived promptly at three o'clock. When Meagan opened the door to him, she found him looking around the partial wraparound porch. She wasn't worried. The cottage was in good shape, and the neighborhood always well kept. He'd find nothing to be critical about there.

"Good afternoon, Mr. Brooks." She hoped she didn't sound too nervous.

He turned back to the front door with a smile. "Good afternoon, Miss Snow. How are you this beautiful spring day?"

Meagan had barely noticed how sunny and warm the day had become. She'd been too busy getting ready for his visit. But she didn't want to appear too apprehensive. "I'm quite well, thank you. Please, come in."

"Welcome to our home, Mr. Brooks," her mother said from behind her. "Meagan has much to show you."

"Thank you, Mrs. Snow. I'm anxious to see Miss Snow's work." He handed his calling card to her and then turned to Meagan. "Did you, perhaps, fashion the frock you are wearing?"

"Yes, I did." Meagan turned slowly, her arms outstretched so that he could see how the skirt was draped.

He nodded. "It's a lovely dress."

"We're both wearing afternoon dresses that she designed herself," Elsie said, turning gracefully so that Mr. Brooks could see how the skirt of her dress draped across the front and tied on the left side.

"These are both quite nice. What else can you show me?"

Meagan led him into the parlor where they'd laid out the rest of her work. She motioned for him to move around the room. "I've made more, but they were for other people and I didn't have time to ask if we could borrow them."

"No need. I wasn't expecting to see this much." He walked over to the frocks she'd made for Becca. "You make children's clothing, too?"

"Of course," Meagan said.

"I have a six-year-old, and she's been growing quite fast. I'm going to have to replenish her wardrobe soon. These look every bit as nice as anything we've had made for her. Since my wife passed away, her family has been helping me choose her clothing."

Meagan wasn't sure what to say—or even how she felt about the fact that he wasn't married. While she felt badly for him and his child, she couldn't deny that knowing he was a widower made it easier to accept the fact that she found him quite attractive.

He smiled. "My Natalie is very vocal about what she likes to wear. I'm sure that together, she and I could manage her wardrobe."

"I'm sure you could, too."

Mr. Brooks looked everything over carefully and listened as Meagan pointed out a certain style or a special drape or ruffle on each outfit she showed him, from school dresses to walking dresses, to Sunday dresses she'd made for her sisters.

"While Meagan is showing you around, I'm going to put

on a pot of water to heat. I hope you'll join us for afternoon tea after you are through here, Mr. Brooks."

"I'd love to, Mrs. Snow." He smiled at her mother and then turned to Meagan. "Let's see the rest."

It was hard to tell what he was thinking, but that he could tell the quality of the fabrics and trim she'd used and commented on the quality of her work gave her hope.

Meagan had just finished showing Mr. Brooks the rest of her work when the front door flew open and Becca and Sarah burst in from school. They stopped short when they saw the banker in the parlor.

"Oh!" Becca said.

"It is all right, Becca. Girls, this is Mr. Brooks. He's the banker who came to see my work."

"Mr. Brooks, these are my sisters. Sarah is the older one, and Becca the younger."

Both sisters gave a quick curtsy, making Meagan smile with pride at their good manners. "How do you do, Mr. Brooks?" Sarah said.

He smiled and bowed from the waist. "Sarah and Becca, is it?"

Becca giggled and bobbed her head.

"It is nice to meet you both. Your sister is a very talented dressmaker and she's made you some lovely things."

"Oh, we know," Sarah said. "She's a wonderful seamstress."

Sarah could be quite outspoken at times, and Meagan was afraid she'd ask outright if he was going to loan them money. "Mama is in the kitchen, making tea for us. Would you girls go let her know that we are ready?"

They hesitated only a moment, just long enough for Meagan to incline her head in the direction of the kitchen. "Please?"

It was obvious that Sarah wanted to stay, but she sighed

and nodded her head, pulling Becca, who was no more anxious to leave the room than she was, with her.

"I'm sorry. They are—"

"They want to know my decision almost as much as you and your mother, I'm sure. That is quite natural. They live here, too, and all of this affects them as well. Why don't we go have that tea and talk about it?"

"Yes, of course," Meagan said. "Please follow me."

"Do you have any sketches of your designs that I could look at?"

"I do. I meant to give my sketch pad to you. I'll get it while Mama pours your tea."

She led him down the hall to the back parlor. It was cozy and bright, and her mother was sitting in her chair, the tea tray in front of her.

"Mr. Brooks, I'm so glad you could join us; please take a seat anywhere you'd like," Mama said. She poured him a cup of tea. "Would you like cream and sugar?"

He sat down in the chair on the other side of her. "Yes, please." He took the proffered cup and took a sip.

"Mama, I forgot my drawings; I'll be right back," Meagan said. By the time she returned, Mr. Brooks seemed right at home. Becca was serving him a tea cake, and he was smiling.

Meagan took the cup of tea her mother had prepared for her and handed the banker her designs.

"Thank you, Miss Snow." He plopped the rest of the tea cake in his mouth and opened her sketchbook. He turned the pages slowly and looked over each design carefully. "This is the frock you have on, isn't it?"

"Yes, it is." He had a good eye for fashion, but he still hadn't given any indication as to what he was going to do.

He closed the sketch pad, handed it to Meagan, and

smiled. "Relax, ladies. I'm very impressed with Miss Snow's designs and the quality of her work. Your front parlor is amply big enough to turn into a shop. I'm going to give you the loan."

For the first time that day, Meagan felt her smile was genuine. "Oh, thank you, Mr. Brooks. You won't be sorry!"

Her mother was up out of her chair, pumping the banker's hand up and down. "Thank you, thank you. Have no worries. We will pay back every penny."

Sarah was barely able to contain her excitement, and Becca was clapping and jumping up and down with excitement.

Mr. Brooks chuckled. "I am not worried. With the support system you have here, I have no doubt that you will make your business a success."

Meagan looked at her mother and sisters. She had a feeling they all helped him make his decision. She nodded. "I'm blessed, that's for certain."

"Come into the bank tomorrow morning, and we'll get your signature." He pulled out a piece of paper and handed it to Meagan. "This is a list of building contractors I think you can trust to do the work you need. I'll need to approve the plans you come up with, of course, but you can rest easy tonight. You have the loan."

Meagan took the paper from him, and as her fingers brushed his, she was taken aback by the electrical jolt that shot up her arm. Her gaze met his and she wondered if he'd felt the same thing.

three

The next day, the receptionist jumped to her feet as soon as Meagan and her mother approached her desk. "Mrs. Snow, Miss Snow, Mr. Brooks has been expecting you. Please, come right this way." The woman smiled and led them to his office.

He seated them once again and put Meagan and her mother both at ease with his smile. Meagan didn't like the way her heartbeat sped up at that smile, though. He was such a nice man and—

"It's not often I feel as good about a loaning money out as I do today," Nate Brooks said as he took his seat behind his desk. He handed Meagan a card. "Be sure to have some business cards made up and leave them wherever you go. This company is known to do beautiful cards at a reasonable price."

"Thank you," Meagan said, taking the small card from him. "I'll go see them this week."

"Well, ladies, let's get started. The sooner we get this paperwork done, the sooner you'll be able to start your business."

For the next half hour, papers passed back and forth as signatures were put to them. Meagan had a moment's misgiving when her mother handed over the deed to their home. If only they'd been able to secure a loan without putting up their home as collateral. It was all very sobering. Her family's future was at stake. If she failed in this endeavor, they could lose their home.

Mr. Brooks seemed to sense her mood. "I believe you are going to build a thriving business, Miss Snow. Otherwise, I wouldn't be lending you the money. I don't do business like that. Try to think of it as placing your deed in my hands for safekeeping."

"I'll try," Meagan said. She wanted to believe him, but she sent up a silent prayer to the One who knew for sure what kind of man Mr. Brooks was. *Lord, please let him be telling the truth. . .that he believes in us and that our deed is in a safe place. I pray that I can make this business successful so that my family won't have to worry about the future, so that Mama can quit working at the Crescent very soon, and so that we can pay back this debt and get our deed back. Please help me, Father.*

When they had signed the last paper and seen for themselves the amount of money that had been put in their account, Meagan and her mother breathed a sigh of relief. It was going to be all right. The Lord would see them through.

Mr. Brooks stood up. "When do you think you'll be contacting the contractor? Did you decide who you might use?"

"I thought I'd go see Mr. Adams. One of our neighbors gave him a very good recommendation, just as you did."

"He is a good man. If he has time, you won't be disappointed in his work."

"We'll go see him first, then."

Mr. Brooks saw them out of his office. "I'll be checking in from time to time to see if you need anything, if it is all right with you."

"Of course." How could she tell him no? His bank had just loaned them a substantial amount of money. She expected him to take an interest in the business.

"I'll be seeing you, then. Good day, ladies."

"Good day, Mr. Brooks. Thank you for your help."

He bowed slightly. "It's been my pleasure."

Meagan and her mother left the bank and lost no time in going to Mr. Adams's business to ask him about turning their parlor into a dressmaking shop. His place wasn't all that far from where they lived, just over Owen Street near the Josephine Hotel, so he agreed to come out the next morning to look around and discuss the needed changes to their home. They bade him good-bye, and Meagan's mother went on to work at the Crescent.

Meagan stopped at home to put a roast in the oven for a celebration supper, and then she hurried back downtown to do some shopping. First, she ordered a new Singer sewing machine and a large folding screen to put in one corner of the room, so that her clients would be able to change for their fittings.

Next, she went to her favorite dry-goods store to order yard goods she wanted to have on hand. She also ordered fabric samples in case what she had in the shop or could find in town didn't suit a client. She bought spools of thread, buttons, trims, and everything else she could think of that she might need. Her fabrics would take several weeks to come in, but she arranged for the other things to be delivered to the house. She couldn't remember when she'd ever had more fun shopping in her life.

❧

"How do I look, Papa?" Natalie Brooks asked Nate. He watched her twirl around and give a cute curtsy. Thankful that he had a housekeeper to help him—he'd never be able to put Natalie's hair up in those curls—he took his daughter's hand in his and bowed to her.

"You look lovely this morning, my dear."

"And you look quite handsome, Papa."

"Thank you. I believe it is time to go to church." Nate helped his daughter with her light cloak, and they headed outside. He assisted her into the runabout and took his own seat. It was a beautiful day. Some of the oaks were beginning to leaf out, and the sky was a clear, cloudless blue. He looked down at his daughter and smiled. "This is the day which the Lord hath made; we will rejoice and be glad in it!"

"Yes, let's, Papa!"

"Are you ready?" Nate asked.

Natalie nodded and grinned. "I am."

"So am I!"

With a flick of Nate's wrist, they were on their way to church. He knew many people in Eureka Springs, either from doing business with them or through his late wife's family. Natalie waved right along with him each time they were greeted by the passengers of a passing buggy.

They were among the last to arrive at church, and Nate and Natalie hurried down the aisle to sit with the Connors family.

"Good morning, Nate," Abigail said with a smile.

"Good morning. We are running a little late this morning."

"No matter," Georgette Connors said, motioning for Natalie to come sit by her. The Connors family gathered his daughter into their circle immediately.

Georgette Connors hugged her close. "You look lovely today, dear. We're having your favorite Sunday dinner."

Natalie looked at her and asked, "We're having roast chicken and apple pie?"

Her grandfather, Jacob Connors, nodded and chuckled. "Well, I like the chicken, but the pie is my favorite."

"It is my favorite, too, Grandfather. But we can't have it until last."

"I know." Jacob shook his head.

Nate sometimes wished that he didn't feel he had to sit with the Connors family, but they were the only relatives Natalie had besides him. His parents had passed away before she was born, and she adored her grandparents and her aunt Abigail. That they loved her could never be in doubt. And Nate wanted them in her life; he just didn't always want them in his. But he didn't know how to separate his life from theirs—wasn't even sure it was possible. Still, they were family, and he enjoyed their affection and care, too. He supposed he should be counting his blessings instead of wishing for more. He wasn't sure what had him so unsettled lately—

"Mama, there seems to be a crowd today," a familiar voice said from behind him. "I hope we don't take someone else's seat."

"Well, if we do, they are later than we are. Besides, we don't pay for them, Meagan. God just wants us here. He doesn't care where we sit."

Nate chuckled silently. Mrs. Snow was a very practical woman. As the family slipped into the row behind him, he could see from the corner of his eye that it was indeed the Snow family.

The service began, and Nate tried to concentrate on it. The singing lifted him up as always and the prayers touched his soul. The sermon about reaching out to others and helping them spoke to his heart. He couldn't help but think of the Snow women sitting behind him, and he prayed that their endeavor would be a success, not because they owed the bank money but because they seemed to be a lovely family without a man to lead them, and his heart went out to them.

As soon as the service was over, Nate stood and turned to

the women behind him. "Good day, Mrs. Snow, Miss Snow. How nice to have you visit with us today."

"Why, Mr. Brooks. I thought that was you," Mrs. Snow said. "Thank you for the welcome, but we aren't visitors. We've been coming here ever since we moved to Eureka Springs."

"Oh, my. I am sorry." Nate felt awful. How had he not noticed that they attended the same church?

"Don't worry about it. We usually sit toward the back," Meagan Snow said. She looked exceptionally lovely in one of the frocks she'd shown him this past week.

"Papa, who are these ladies you are talking to?" Natalie asked, tugging at his sleeve.

"These are nice ladies I met through the bank, Natalie. They are going to be starting a new dressmaking shop. Mrs. Snow, Miss Snow, this is my daughter, Natalie."

"Why, hello, Natalie, how nice to meet you."

"I'm pleased to meet you, ma'am," Natalie said, looking curiously at the family.

As his in-laws turned from talking to the people in the pew in front of them, Nate made the introductions all around, from Mrs. Snow and her daughters to the Connorses and back again. Jacob and Georgette were gracious, but Nate wasn't pleased when Abigail practically brushed the introductions aside by only saying, "Pleased, I am sure."

She nudged him to move out of the row and said in a loud whisper, "We need to hurry, Nate, dear. You know how Mama gets upset if we dawdle. She likes us to be on time for Sunday dinner."

Nate didn't know what she was talking about. Georgette had never acted upset about how long they stayed after church. She usually did her own socializing before they left. As the rest of the Connorses followed Abigail out into the aisle, he wasn't sure what to say. "Natalie and I will be along shortly."

Abigail sighed. "Very well. Try to hurry, though."

Nate was at a loss as to what to say to the Snow family. "I...ah..."

"Oh, we quite understand, Mr. Brooks," Meagan said, and he had a feeling she was trying to ease his discomfort at his sister-in-law's rudeness. "We have a Sunday dinner to take out of the oven, too."

Nate and Natalie walked down the aisle with the Snow ladies. He could see that Abigail looked a bit put out as she left with her parents, but he wasn't inclined to hurry on her account. He wasn't inclined to hurry at all.

❧

Abigail fairly fumed on the way out of church. Who were those women Nate was being so friendly to? Oh, he'd said that they were going to open a dressmaking shop, but how exactly did he know them? The way they looked at him, you'd think they were old friends. The oldest daughter—what was her name? All she could remember was their last name was Snow. Most likely, Nate was still talking to them. That thought didn't sit well with her. She knew nearly everyone Nate socialized with, and she'd never seen these women. She didn't like the way Nate had looked at the oldest daughter, either. She didn't like it at all.

Abigail wasn't the least bit happy that Nate hesitated when she suggested that they leave. He always left with them—usually she rode back to her parents' home with him, and Natalie rode with her parents. But not today. He didn't suggest it, and she wasn't going to wait on him.

Her mother looked at her closely as they rode home in their buggy but didn't say anything until they were home and in her kitchen. "Abigail, dear, what is wrong? You seem quite out of sorts. And what was all of that about my being upset if Nate isn't on time. I'm not like that, and you well know it!"

"I'm sorry, Mother. I just know how much you put into preparing Sunday dinner before you go to church. It isn't right for you to have to keep it warm."

"Dear, it is no problem to keep dinner warm. The chicken will be fine until Nate and Natalie get here, and I still need to cream the potatoes and warm the bread."

"I don't know why you let your help have Sunday off when you always have company over, Mama."

"I don't need Laura on Sundays, Abigail. I think she should be able to go to church with her family the same as I do. Besides, I didn't always have help, and I don't want to forget completely how to cook. And you let your housekeeper off."

"Well, yes, most times I do. But I'm here most of the day or out with friends." Abigail did count herself very lucky. She'd received a substantial inheritance from her paternal grandparents and the house from her mother's mother. With that, and the fact that her papa had invested wisely, she was independently wealthy in her own right, even without what she would inherit from her parents one day. She'd been used to wealth all of her life, unlike her mother, who married into it. Abigail sighed. She really had no choice but to offer to lend a hand. "Well, what can I do to help? It appears Nate is going to keep us waiting all afternoon."

"Dear, he'll be along any minute. He really hasn't kept us waiting."

Abigail sighed. *Oh, yes, Mama, he has. He's kept me waiting for a very long time. I've been patient way too long. It is time to find a way to persuade him to marry me. . .and not just for*

Natalie's sake, but for my own. If I wait too much longer, it might be too late. I must find a way.

Nate wasn't sure what kind of welcome he was going to get when they arrived at the Connorses' home, but he really wasn't that much later than usual. He lifted Natalie up so that she could use the knocker and let her grandparents know that they had arrived.

"We're here!" Natalie said as her grandfather let them in.

"That you are. Are you hungry?" her grandfather asked.

"I am!" She sniffed. "It smells really good in here!"

"It does, doesn't it?" Jacob said. "I'm a bit on the hungry side, too."

Georgette and Abigail came in from the dining room. "Well, it's about time!" Abigail said. Nate knew she wasn't upset with Natalie, but he didn't like that she'd managed to take the smile off his daughter's face.

"It's not Natalie's fault, Abigail."

"Oh, I know that." She gave him a look that told him she was not pleased with him at all. He just wasn't sure why. They really weren't that late.

"We hurried, Aunt Abby. Honest we did."

"There just was a clog-up getting out of the building." Nate turned to his hostess. "I'm sorry if we've held things up, Mother Connors. Is there anything I can do?"

"It isn't a problem, Nate dear. Really. Abigail is just having a bad day. We rarely get things on the table until one o'clock, and it's not even that now. Natalie, would you like to come help finish up?"

"Oh, yes!" Natalie said, following her grandmother to the kitchen.

"Nate, come tell me about your week while our women get

dinner on the table," Jacob called.

Nate looked from Abigail to her papa, shrugged, and followed Jacob to the drawing room. Some days there was no pleasing Abigail, and he'd learned not to worry overly much about it. He certainly wasn't going to start now.

four

Nate was glad for Monday to arrive. Abigail had been decidedly cool all through Sunday dinner, and he didn't enjoy being around her at all when she was in that kind of mood. The Connors parents had talked him into letting Natalie stay the afternoon with the promise to bring her home after supper, and Nate had been glad to take off. He'd tried to relax and read his Bible for a while when he got home, but he kept thinking about Meagan Snow and her family. He still couldn't quite understand how they'd been attending the same church all this time without him knowing it. Yet he supposed there really was no reason he would have known them had he not begun doing business with them.

As he headed to work on Monday morning, Nate reflected that, most Sundays, he spoke to the people who sat around them and then hurried off to the Connors home for Sunday dinner. He couldn't remember when he'd done things any differently until yesterday. That was probably why Abigail was upset with him. With reason, he supposed, as she most often rode with him after church. She could have done so yesterday, too. He'd been polite to people doing business with her father's bank. It was what he was supposed to be doing.

Later that Monday, he told himself it was what he should do when he went to check on how things were going at the Snow home. Meagan had told him that Mr. Adams was going to start on the renovations today, and he wanted to see firsthand how it was going. Mr. Adams's work wagon was outside, and Nate was sure he was still hard at work.

"Mr. Brooks, please come in," Meagan said as she opened the door. "Mr. Adams has been working all day!" Her eyes sparkled with excitement as she led him into the parlor. The older man stopped working and came to shake his hand.

"Miss Snow said you'd recommended me, and I thank you for it, Mr. Brooks."

"You're welcome. It looks like you are making good headway." Nate entered the parlor to see that the carpenter was building shelves all along one wall, where Miss Snow could store her sewing supplies.

They'd also decided to turn one of the side windows into an entry door, and Mr. Adams would be installing that by the end of the week. "I should have everything Miss Snow asked for finished by the middle of March," the man said.

Nate nodded. He knew Adams would keep his word; that was the main reason he'd recommended him.

"It is looking great, isn't it, Mr. Brooks?" Meagan asked.

"It is. I think you are going to have a lovely shop here, Miss Snow." She was the one who was lovely. Her hair was upswept, and the afternoon dress she wore was one of the ones he'd admired the day he'd inspected her work. It was made of a blue and cream stripe that brought out the color of her eyes. Her cheeks were flushed pink, and he was sure it was from the excitement of seeing her plans come to life.

"Thank you. I already have a few orders even before the shop opens. Of course, they are from friends and neighbors. But they wanted to be the first to be able to say they bought from our shop. I'll be getting clothing labels to put inside all my work soon, and these dresses will be the first to have them."

"But the shop isn't quite ready."

"No. But I have my old sewing machine set up in the dining room. I don't want to lose any time. And these ladies will be wonderful to spread word about the shop opening."

"Sometimes that's the best kind of advertising."

"That's what I thought. I've had flyers and business cards made up to leave with some of the dry-goods stores for people who ask about seamstresses, and I've paid for some newspaper advertising to come out the day the shop opens."

"It seems you've thought things through. I'm sure you will build up your clientele in no time." As he spoke, Nate reminded himself to urge Abigail and her friends to give Miss Snow some business. They spent untold money on their wardrobes. Surely, they'd be glad to know there was a new dressmaker in town. As far as that went, his daughter needed new clothes, too. Even though Abigail and her mother had seen to having Natalie's clothes made, he was her father, after all. "I'd like to bring my daughter around to see you. She's growing so fast these days, and I'm sure you could help us choose some styles and fabrics that she would love."

"I would be honored to make something for your little girl, Mr. Brooks."

"When would be a good time for you to see us?"

"Whenever it is convenient for you," Meagan said.

"I'll wait until the shop is open and bring her in then."

"Wonderful! She can be one of my first clients. I'll pull out some of my most recent ladies' magazines and patterns and designs, and we'll see what she might like."

"She'll love that," Nate said.

"Why, Mr. Brooks. How nice to see you," Mrs. Snow said on entering the house. He supposed she was coming in from work. She peeked inside the parlor to see the work that had been completed. "Isn't it all so exciting?"

"It is that. I wanted to see what Mr. Adams had done and was talking to Miss Snow about bringing my daughter in to see her. She is in need of some new things, and I am sure your daughter can please her."

"Oh, I'm sure she will. Meagan will listen carefully to what your little girl likes and will come up with some beautiful ideas."

"I'm certain of it." Nate pulled his watch out of his pocket. "I'd better be leaving now. I'll be back to see how things are going, and if you need anything, please don't hesitate to get in touch with me."

"Oh, we won't," Meagan assured him. "You've helped us so much, aside from approving our loan. With Papa gone, it gives us peace of mind to know that we can come to you for advice."

Nate felt a swell of pride at her words. It felt very good to feel needed. "I'm more than pleased to help. And Miss Snow?"

"Yes?"

"Your papa would have been very proud of you and your mother's decisions, I am sure."

Meagan ducked her head, but not before he saw a tear spring to her eyes. "Thank you."

"I've been trying to tell her how proud her papa would be, Mr. Brooks. Thank you for your kind words."

"You're very welcome."

⁂

Over the next few weeks, Meagan began to look forward to Nate's visits. Just when he'd become Nate to her, she couldn't say, but somewhere along the way, they'd begun to call each other by their first names. As she began to stock the shelves that Mr. Adams had just finished that morning, she found herself humming and wondering if Nate would be by that afternoon.

He'd been visiting often to check on the work being done, and while Meagan couldn't wait to open her shop, she was afraid she wouldn't be seeing much of Nate once she did. Her humming stopped, and then she remembered that he was bringing in his daughter, Natalie, once the shop opened. She would be seeing him at least some after the opening. That was set for the very next Monday, March 22. She shivered with excitement as she put a bolt of copper silk atop a bolt of nutmeg brown brocade. She stepped back and looked at the bolts of fabric she'd arranged by color. They were the latest colors and fabrics, and they'd just come in on the train the day before. More and more, her family parlor was taking on the look of a real dressmaker's shop.

Not only had Mr. Adams made shelves to hold her fabrics, he'd also made drawers for all her notions and trims. He'd put the most beautiful glass-windowed door in the place where a full-length window had been. The man was a wonderful craftsman, and he took into account all of her suggestions and ideas. But he'd be through here before long. He'd be moving his work outside tomorrow, as they'd decided to have him paint the porch railing to freshen it up.

Meagan's new sewing machine had come in, too, and it was set up in front of the south-facing bay window where she'd have good light all day and could see anyone coming up to the shop. It was so easy to use, she'd almost finished the frocks that had been ordered before Mr. Adams had begun transforming their parlor.

She loved her shop. It was coming together even better than she'd imagined. Their own settee and two chairs with round tables sat in the front of the shop where her clients could look at the ladies' magazines and fashion plates and the sketches of her own designs. The settee had been recovered in a rose damask and looked lovely. She and her mother decided that she needed two screens in case she was taking measurements of a customer and another came in at the same time for a fitting. Meagan could only hope she'd become that busy. But just in case, and so they'd both be alike, she'd ordered another screen. It had come in today, and Mr. Adams had put both screens up in opposite corners. She only had to organize and put up her trims and notions to have everything in place.

Mr. Adams had hung a bell above the shop door to alert Meagan to arriving customers, and she turned in surprise now as it rang. Nate Brooks entered with a smile on his face, and Meagan's heart felt all fluttery as it always did when she first saw him. She'd been trying to tell herself to quit being so silly, but she really had no control over the way her heart beat faster in his presence.

"Good afternoon, Meagan. Mr. Adams said he thought you were in the shop."

She loved the way he said her name. "Good afternoon, Nate. I've lost track of time today, but look how much I accomplished!" She swept her arm around the room. "Isn't it looking wonderful?"

His deep laugh had her heart doing a little flip. "It is. Mr. Adams says he's nearly through here, and I can see that he is. It looks as if you are ready to open today."

"Oh, I still have some things to be delivered from the dry-goods store, and Mr. Adams has the railings to finish up. I actually could open now, but we want to make sure everything is as clean as it can be. We'll have it completely ready on Monday. I'll use the extra time this week to finish up the frocks I've been working on."

"I'm sure your open house will be very successful. I'm handing out the cards you gave me. Perhaps I should wait until the next day to bring Natalie. Although, she is so excited I hate to disappoint her."

"Why don't you bring her tomorrow and then again on Monday for the open house, so that she can enjoy that? If you bring her in early, I'll be able to give her my undivided attention. And she can be the first real customer to come to the shop."

"Oh, she would love that! Thank you for suggesting it, Meagan. Will this time tomorrow be all right?"

"Of course it will be. Or you could bring her a little later—whatever works with your schedule."

"How about around four thirty, is that too late?"

"That would be fine."

"Wonderful. I'll have the housekeeper bring Natalie to the bank, and we'll come over from there. I'm not going to tell her until tomorrow, though. It will be a great surprise for her."

"I look forward to it," Meagan said.

Nate nodded. "Yes, well, everything seems to be going according to plan. I'm very happy for you. And I hope that your mother will be able to quit her position at the Crescent before too long, as I know that is your wish."

"I pray that she will be able to," Meagan said as she saw him out. "And thank you for your consideration of her."

"You're welcome. I'll see you tomorrow."

Meagan watched him leave and was glad she hadn't gone back inside when he turned and gave her a wave from the street. She'd come to like Nate Brooks quite a bit in the last few weeks.

☙

The next afternoon, Meagan watched from the window and saw Nate with his daughter as they came up the walk. They went around to the shop door and used the knocker instead of just entering.

"Good day." Meagan opened the door for them.

"Natalie, do you remember Miss Snow from church?"

"Yes, Papa, I do. She's pretty."

Meagan could feel the color flood her face.

"Yes, she is," Nate said.

"Why, thank you." She was glad Natalie was there so that she didn't have to look at Nate. "You are very pretty yourself."

Natalie giggled. "Thank you. Papa says you make beautiful clothing and that you are going to make something for me."

"I am, if you think you might like some of my ideas."

"Oh, I'm sure that I will," the little girl said.

"Well, let's go sit down, and I'll show you some of the new styles and find out what you like and don't like."

The child followed her and took a seat on the settee, where her father joined her. Meagan had only seen Natalie briefly that day in church. Since then, she and her family had sat in the back where they usually did. And normally, they left right after church, before Nate and his daughter came up the aisle. Natalie looked a lot like her father with her dark hair and brown eyes, and she seemed very sweet.

Meagan pulled out several ladies' magazines. She looked at Natalie and asked, "What is it you need right now?"

"I would like a new walking dress, and I heard Aunt Abby tell Grandmother just the other day that I could use a new Sunday dress."

Meagan looked at Nate for guidance.

"I think she could use more than that, but it will be a start."

"That is where we will begin, then," Meagan said. Turning to a page, she showed them some of the newest styles for young girls. One was a walking dress made of a dark blue cashmere and had a finely pleated vest, with three wide rows of pleats at the hem. White lace trimmed the pleated collar and the cuffs.

"Oh, how pretty. Could it be in another color?"

"Of course. We can make it any color you like," Meagan assured her as she turned to another page and showed her a dress of cream foulard with a heavy green band at the hem.

"I like that, too, Miss Snow! I even like the colors," Natalie said.

"I do, too. Let us see what else we can find that you like."

With Nate looking on, Meagan showed his daughter more styles and brought out the newest dresses she'd made for her sisters. By the time they were through, they'd decided on a walking dress and a dress to wear to church. She took Natalie's measurements and gave her some swatches of the fabric in the colors she liked to take home with her. She would let Meagan know which ones she wanted when they came to the grand opening.

When it was time to leave, Nate turned to Meagan. "Natalie quite enjoyed herself today—and I enjoyed watching the two of you decide on the items to add to her wardrobe. If that is the way you are going to treat all of your customers, I have no doubt that you are going to do quite well. No doubt at all."

five

By the end of the next week, Nate could no longer deny that he was very attracted to Meagan Snow. His daughter had taken to her immediately, and he understood why. Meagan was a warm and lovely woman, who treated Natalie as if she was just as special as the wealthiest client she might have. He also liked her family almost as much as he liked her.

He'd waited late in the day of her open house to take Natalie in, not wanting to detract from what Meagan needed to do in trying to obtain clients. Quite a few women were still there. While he hadn't felt out of place in the shop when he'd taken his daughter to meet Meagan, today he did. Meagan greeted them, but with so many women to serve, it was impossible for Natalie to receive the same kind of attention she'd had the first time he brought her in.

Mrs. Snow was helping her daughter, and she must have sensed Nate's discomfort. She came over and offered her hand. "Good afternoon, Mr. Brooks, how nice to see you and your daughter again."

"Thank you, Mrs. Snow." He looked around the room and lowered his voice. "It appears that the open house is a success. I think I should bring Natalie in another day to discuss her fabric choices."

"Oh no, Meagan would feel terrible if you do that. She doesn't want to disappoint Natalie. The shop is due to close shortly. Why don't you and your daughter come out to the kitchen with me? I just took some cookies out of the oven, but it is so close to closing I don't believe we are going to need them."

"Oh, please, Papa," Natalie said with the look that rarely failed to get a yes out of him. "I want to show Miss Snow the colors I decided on."

Nate nodded, and before long, he and Natalie were sitting at the kitchen table, eating warm cookies and watching Mrs. Snow start dinner. She reminded him of his mother. Becca and Sarah took Natalie under their wing, and Nate listened to them talk about school and church and any number of other things until Meagan rushed into the kitchen.

"I am so sorry, Natalie. I wasn't expecting so many people."

"It appeared to be a great success." Nate smiled at Meagan. Her face was flushed, and she was smiling. One only had to look at her to realize that it had been a very good day for her and that she was very happy.

She nodded. "I have appointments set up for the rest of the week with ladies who want to order some of their spring wardrobe from me! But I would love to see what fabrics you've chosen for your dresses, Natalie."

"Why don't you and Natalie go do that now? Supper will be ready in about a half hour, and Mr. Brooks and Natalie can join us."

"Oh, we can't intrude like that, Mrs. Snow," Nate said, although the smell of the stew she was stirring had his mouth watering.

"You won't be intruding. We would like your company. Unless you are due to be somewhere else?"

Nate shook his head. "No, we aren't." He'd told his housekeeper not to worry about dinner, that he would take Natalie to her favorite restaurant for dinner. Sharing a meal with the Snow women seemed a much better choice.

"Please, Papa," Natalie said. Apparently his daughter agreed with him.

"Thank you, Mrs. Snow. We gladly accept your invitation."

He couldn't remember the last time he had such an enjoyable evening. He watched as Meagan and Natalie discussed the colors and styles. By the time they'd settled on everything, Mrs. Snow was calling them to supper in the dining room. The table had been set with china and lit with both candles and gaslight. The atmosphere was warm and inviting.

Once seated, Mrs. Snow asked Nate to say the prayer.

He gladly obliged. "Dear Father, we thank You for this day and for the many blessings You've bestowed upon us. We thank You for the food we are about to eat. Most of all we thank You for Your Son and our Savior. In His name we pray. Amen."

He totally enjoyed the informality of the simple meal. The beef stew was well seasoned and served with a fresh salad. For dessert, they were treated to bread pudding. Nate was amazed that Mrs. Snow, even with the help of her daughters, could prepare such a meal and set so nice a table without the aid of hired help. Perhaps he'd been around the Connors family too long.

ಎ

During the rest of March, Nate and Natalie visited Meagan's shop often, usually on a Saturday, but sometimes during the week. They had the first fitting of the first dress, then more fittings. By the time they arrived at the shop, Mrs. Snow, whom he'd found didn't work on the weekends, was usually taking a pan of cookies, a cake, or a pie out of the oven. She never failed to ask them if they wanted some of whatever she'd baked.

On the weekday fittings, they almost always were asked to

stay for dinner, and Nate thought he would have agreed to stay even if it wasn't for his daughter's pleading expression. He enjoyed being there as much as Natalie did. It was more than a little refreshing to see how the Snow family had coped with the loss of a husband, father, and breadwinner. They might have had household staff at some point, judging from the home and the furnishings. They talked about Mr. Snow often, and Nate could tell they loved him and missed him greatly, but they honored his memory by getting on with their lives the best they could. He never heard them complain. Maybe he related so well to them because they'd suffered a loss just as he did when he lost his wife, Rose, in the fire.

Whatever the reason, he liked being around the Snow family. He didn't feel that he had to be constantly on guard as he did most times with Rose's family. He supposed that was because he'd always felt guilty that he hadn't been able to save her. By the time he'd reached their home, it was engulfed in flames, and Abigail was outside holding Natalie. He'd tried to go in, but some of his neighbors had stopped him. In shock, all he could do was join Abigail, taking his daughter in his arms as they watched the flames.

Something died in him that day, but he'd struggled through, questioning God, reading and praying—and doing his best to raise the daughter he adored. He knew now that the Lord had never left his side, and while he still wondered why his Rose had to die, he knew she was in a better place. He strived to raise Natalie the way he thought Rose would want him to. . .trusting in the Lord to help him.

Since he'd met Meagan Snow and her family, he'd felt more alive than he had since the day of the fire. And it felt really good to be looking forward rather than backward.

"Papa, do you like the Snow family as much as I do?" Natalie asked when they were on their way to the shop for a fitting of her new Sunday dress.

He looked down and smiled at his daughter. She was always in a good mood when they were on their way to the Snows' home. "Well, I'm not sure how much that is, but I do like them very much."

"They are so nice, and they like to talk to me, and I like talking to them. I just enjoy being there. It's very. . .homey, isn't it?"

That is it, exactly, Nate thought. "Yes, it is."

"I like being there almost as much as at home. . .and much better than any other place."

As she skipped and chattered alongside him, Nate realized that Natalie was always very happy and talkative when they left the Snow home, but she didn't have much to say when she left her aunt Abigail's. He began to wonder why that was. Natalie had always been close to Abigail, but not quite as open or happy around her aunt as she was around Meagan. Maybe it was a difference in personalities. Or perhaps it could be the different way each woman treated her. Abigail sometimes treated Natalie as if she were younger than she really was, and Meagan treated her. . .like a person in her own right. Nate shook his head. Mulling it over wasn't telling him anything. Perhaps his daughter just liked Meagan better than she did Abigail. *That* he could certainly understand.

❧

Meagan began looking forward to Natalie's fittings more each time she came in. Her heart went out to the child and her papa. It had been so hard for Meagan's family when her own father had passed away, but how very hard it must be for Nate to raise a child on his own, or for Natalie to barely remember her mother. Yet Natalie was a delightful child and a joy to have around.

Nate, however, made her pulse race and her heart beat faster these days. Something about the man's slow smile never failed to make her smile back—and her heart seemed to do little flip-flops at the sight of him. He was such a gentleman, and he treated her mother and sisters with a gentle grace that touched her heart. He was extra nice to her mother, and that meant so much to Meagan. More than likely, his own loss made him relate to them and be so considerate. Whatever it was, she found her respect growing for him each day—as well as her attraction to him. She tried not to show how she felt and lived in fear that she wouldn't be able to hide those feelings much longer.

At this fitting, she concentrated on Natalie and how well the new suit dress fit. It was in the child's favorite colors, blue with green trim. Its bodice was fitted, and the skirt was tucked in the front and pulled to the rear to form a modified bustle, nothing the size of what women were wearing these days, but enough of one to make Natalie feel she was wearing the latest style. The collar and cuffs on the dress matched the green inserts of the jacket. To Meagan, Natalie looked adorable.

Apparently, Nate thought so, too.

"You do wonderful work, Meagan. Nothing we've had made for Natalie in the last few years can compare to the quality of your work."

"Thank you. I love doing this. I am so happy you made it possible. I talked Mama into giving her notice at the Crescent. Today is her last day."

"Oh, I'm happy to hear that news!"

"Somehow, I thought you might be."

Nate nodded. "Your mother reminds me of my own at times. I'm glad she will be able to stay at home again."

"I convinced her that I'd be needing her help here. I do think the business will grow enough that I will need some extra hands. I hope so, anyway."

"Once word gets out from the ladies you are sewing for now, you'll need her."

Natalie had been turning this way and that in front of the mirror. "I love this dress, Miss Meagan! I can't wait to wear it. When do you think it will be ready?"

"You may take it home with you."

Natalie clapped. "I can wear it on Sunday. Oh, I can hardly wait!"

"I look forward to seeing you in it," Meagan said.

"I can't wait to see what Grandmother and Aunt Abby say! I haven't told them about it because I wanted it to be a surprise."

Nate chuckled. "They certainly will be surprised, mostly because you and I did this without their help."

He sounded proud that he'd been the one to help his daughter, but Meagan wondered if his in-laws would feel the same way. She'd watched them in church more than she should have, she supposed. It was obvious that Nate's sister-in-law wanted everyone to think she had some kind of claim on him. Perhaps she did. If so, Meagan needed to quit weaving daydreams about the man. Perhaps she needed to assume that he was taken, for even if he wasn't, she'd be silly to think that a man like him would be interested in her.

six

When he and Natalie went to dinner at Abigail's the first Saturday evening in April, Nate was still wondering about Natalie's differing moods when with Abigail or the Snows. It wasn't that Natalie didn't want to be with her aunt—she was excited to be spending the night there.

Abigail had also invited her parents, which was a big change from her usual dinner parties, so the evening was more enjoyable than usual for Nate. . .until his parents-in-law went home and Natalie went up to get ready for bed. Then he was left alone with Abigail.

"That was a wonderful meal, Abigail. And it was nice that it was just family tonight."

"I thought so, too," she said, leading him into the front parlor. She took a seat in the ladies' chair flanking the fire-place, and Nate sat down in the gentleman's seat across from her. It was a nice room, elegantly furnished, but he'd never really felt comfortable in it. Now he knew why. It didn't have that homey feel that the Snows' home had. Maybe it was because Abigail lived by herself or because she was too concerned about nothing getting messed.

"Nate, dear," Abigail began, "don't you think it's time you thought of marrying again?"

It had been awhile since she'd brought up the subject, but he'd been expecting it for some time. He answered the way he always did. "No. Natalie and I are getting along quite well. I have a wonderful housekeeper who takes good care of us."

"But don't you get lonesome?"

He had been lonesome for a long time, but only for Rose. Now he realized that thoughts of her had somehow been replaced by Meagan Snow, and he wasn't quite sure how he felt about that.

"Don't you?" Abigail prodded.

"Everyone gets lonesome from time to time, Abigail. Of course I do. That certainly isn't a reason to get married, though. There needs to be more—"

"What about for Natalie's sake? She needs a woman's influence in her life."

Nate chuckled. "She has that. She has you and your mother, and even my housekeeper, who is wonderful with her." She also had the Snow women, but Nate felt it best not to mention them.

"Nate." Abigail had that exasperated tone in her voice. He seemed to bring it out in her. "You know that Rose would have wanted you to remarry, and you know that I love Natalie as my own. I care for you—"

"Abigail, we have this discussion on a regular basis, and I haven't changed my mind. I—"

"Papa, I'm ready for bed," Natalie interrupted, and Nate had never been happier to have a conversation cut short. "Are you going to hear my prayers?"

"I certainly am," Nate said, getting up to follow her upstairs.

Abigail did love Natalie, there was no denying that and never had been. She'd furnished a room specifically for her niece and had chosen everything with the little girl in mind. Nate did appreciate her love for his daughter. But that was all.

Natalie knelt beside the bed as she always did, and Nate knelt next to her as she prayed.

"Dear God, thank You for Papa and for Grandmother and

Grandfather and for Aunt Abby. And thank You for all the Snow ladies, especially Miss Meg. Please watch over them all and keep them safe. Please forgive me for my sins and help me to do Your will. And please let Papa get home safely. Thank You for everything, dear God. In Jesus' name. Amen."

"Amen." Nate echoed. He realized that Natalie must like Meagan a great deal when she called her Miss Meg. She always shortened the first names of the people she cared a lot about.

Natalie jumped into bed, and he helped her pull the quilt up to her neck. He bent down and kissed her brow. "Good night, Natalie."

"Good night, Papa. I'll see you at church tomorrow."

He nodded. "Yes, you will. Sleep tight, and sweet dreams."

"Thank you." Natalie yawned.

Nate met Abigail in the hall. "I'll go in and tell her good night and be right back. Would you like a cup of chocolate before you go?"

Nate didn't want to continue the conversation they'd begun earlier. He shook his head. "No, thank you. I'm quite full from that excellent dinner you served. Thank you again, Abigail. There's no need to see me to the door; I can let myself out."

"Yes, well, all right," Abigail said a bit coolly.

He knew she was unhappy with him, but if he stayed and continued the conversation, her mood would only get worse. "I'll see you and Natalie at church tomorrow." Nate didn't wait for an answer. He hurried down the stairs, gathered his overcoat, and took his leave, shutting the door behind him.

❧

As soon as he arrived at church the next morning, Nate could tell Abigail still wasn't happy. The tightness around her lips had proven over time to be a signal that she was in a bad mood. He decided to ignore her moodiness and hoped she would get over it.

"Good morning!" he said to no one in particular, but with a smile and a wink for his daughter.

"Good morning, Papa," Natalie said, scooting over on the pew to make room for him. "Aunt Abby and Grandmother and Grandfather think my new outfit is beautiful!"

He was almost certain he heard a *huff* coming from Abigail as he replied to his daughter, "You do look quite lovely this morning."

"Thank you. I feel pretty in the dress Miss Meg made me!"

Georgette Connors leaned forward, looking past her daughter and granddaughter to address Nate. "I want to know where to find this new dressmaker you've found. The quality of her work is superb!"

"Her name is Meagan Snow, but you've already met her, Georgette," Nate said. "She and her family attend church here. I introduced you to them."

Georgette look confused and cocked her head to the side. Nate could tell she was trying to remember.

"They sat behind us over a month ago. The bank is financing her new business endeavor."

"Oh, yes. I remember now. Well, I'll talk to you about it later."

Nate nodded. Thankfully, he was on the outside of the row by his daughter and not beside Abigail. She'd barely acknowledged his greeting, and she looked stiff as a board. He had a feeling it was all this talk about Natalie's new dress. She was probably angry that he hadn't consulted her about the addition to his daughter's wardrobe. Well, she would have to get over it.

When the service was over, Nate looked around for the Snow women so that he could point them out to Georgette again, but they were out the door before he could get her attention.

Natalie rode with her grandparents back to their house, and Nate offered Abigail a ride, as she and Natalie had been picked up by her parents that morning.

"Yes, thank you," she accepted a bit coolly.

Nate sighed inwardly. Sometimes he wished they didn't have a standing date to eat with his in-laws every Sunday. He helped Abigail into his surrey and wondered if she was going to tell him why she was angry. He took the reins in hand and flicked his wrist. Once they were moving, Abigail lost no time in letting him know what her problem was.

"Who is this Meg that I've been hearing about from Natalie?"

"Why she's the dressmaker who made her new dress," Nate answered.

"I know that, Nate. But where did she come from, and how do you know about her?"

Nate tried to tamp down his growing irritation that neither Abigail nor her mother remembered meeting the Snows. "You've met her at church, Abigail. I introduced you all back in February."

Her brow furrowed, trying to remember.

Nate sighed. "They were sitting in the pew behind us."

"Oh, yes. Now I remember. But I don't recall you saying she was a seamstress."

"Well, I did. She is a talented dressmaker who's opened her own shop. The bank loaned her the money to get it started—"

"Oh, I see." Abigail sounded a little less cool. "So you are just helping her get started and making sure that our bank gets a return on the investment."

Maybe that's how it had started out, but Nate knew that wasn't the reason he was taking Natalie to Meagan's shop now. There was much more to it, but it wasn't something Abigail would want to hear, and it wasn't anything Nate wanted to tell her. . .not yet, anyway. "I'd appreciate it if you would spread the word about the shop and the quality of Miss Snow's work. A word from you would help a lot."

"I suppose I could do that," Abigail said. But she didn't sound too happy about it.

Nate decided it was time to change the subject. "I received my invitation to the grand opening gala at the Crescent on May 20th."

"Oh, good. I received mine, too. Everyone is talking about how it's going to be the event of the season!"

Nate was sure it would be. He wanted to bring up Meagan and her shop again and how he was sure there would be women wanting new ball gowns. But Abigail's mood had lifted with talk of the Crescent, and for everyone's sake at dinner, he felt it best not to change subjects. Somehow, he managed to keep up with the conversation while his thoughts were on Meagan.

Abigail's assumption that he was taking Natalie to Meagan's shop to insure the success of her business had him facing the truth. He'd come to care for the Snow family, and he wanted the business to be a success for their sake. Yet that wasn't the reason he kept ordering items for his daughter's wardrobe. He was beginning to care for Meagan more each time he was around her. That was why he would keep taking Natalie to Meagan for all of her wardrobe needs. It was that simple.

seven

The next week, Meagan and her mother went to order more fabric and trims. Several of the ladies who'd come in the day she'd opened had ordered afternoon dresses, and one had ordered a dinner gown. Nate had also decided to order several more items for Natalie. Meagan was thrilled, and it did look as if her mother had quit working at the Crescent just in time. There was no doubt she was needed.

Celebrating this change, Meagan and her mother decided to have lunch at the Southern Hotel. Many of the hotels were located near the springs so that their guests wouldn't have to go far to take advantage of what many thought to be healing waters. Being located adjacent to the Basin Spring, the Southern was no exception.

As they entered the hotel, Meagan felt wonderful to be able to treat her mother to a luxury they hadn't been able to afford since Papa's death. The girls were in school, but hopefully, she'd be able to treat them one day soon, too.

After the two ladies were shown to a table in the elegant dining room, a waiter handed them each a menu. Meagan looked it over and ordered a cup of bouillon, an egg sandwich, and tea.

"I'll have the same, please," her mother requested. When the waiter left, she chuckled. "We could just as well have had this meal at home."

"I know, Mama. But we still have more shopping to do, and you deserve a treat."

"Thank you, dear. You've been working so hard so that I could quit working at the Crescent; I think it is you who deserves a treat."

"I know there is nothing wrong with you working outside the home. The Crescent Hotel is beautiful, and I'm sure it is a nice place to work. But Becca is still young, and, well, we all just want you at home," Meagan said. "The house doesn't feel the same if you aren't there."

Her mother reached over and patted her hand. "You are a wonderful daughter, Meagan. I am proud of all my girls, and your papa would be so proud of all of you, too."

"Thank you. We've been very blessed to have parents such as you and Papa. I hope that he would approve of what we—"

"Why, good day, ladies," a voice from over Meagan's shoulder interrupted.

Her mother smiled in recognition, but Meagan knew who it was even before she turned around to see. She'd know that voice anywhere—even if her pounding heart hadn't recognized it. She smiled and said, "Good day, Mr. Brooks."

"We're treating ourselves to celebrate that I can stay at home and help my Meagan," her mother added. "Thank you for making that possible, Mr. Brooks. Would you like to join us?"

Thank you, Mama. Meagan held her breath, waiting for his answer.

"Actually, I would like that, if you are sure?"

"Please do," Meagan's mother said. "We would like the company."

He looked at Meagan for confirmation.

"Please do." She sounded a little breathless to her own ears.

Nate smiled and took a seat. The waiter seemed to come out of nowhere with a menu. Nate brushed it away with a smile and said, "I'll have the gentleman's plate, please. And please add the ladies' ticket to mine."

"Oh, no!" Meagan said. "We can't let you do that."

"After the wonderful meals I've enjoyed at your home? I can't join you if you won't let me pay for your lunch." He half stood before Meagan's mother shook her head and chuckled.

"Please sit, Mr. Brooks. We'll be honored to have lunch with you."

"Good." He sat back down and grinned at Meagan. "It's not often I have the opportunity to have lunch with such lovely ladies."

His glance captured Meagan's, and she could feel the warm rush of color steal up her cheeks. The man had a way of making the blood race through her veins.

He smiled and took a sip from his water glass. "What brought you out and about besides your celebration?"

"We ordered some fabric, and we're going to buy some trim and notions this afternoon. I need trim for the coat you've ordered for Natalie."

"Natalie's grandmother loved the new Sunday dress. I gave her your name and the address of your shop. I'm hoping she and Natalie's aunt Abigail will spread the word about the shop. The women in their circle seem to have a new outfit every time I see them. I've also heard that one of the dressmakers in town is getting married, and everyone is worried that there just aren't enough seamstresses in town. I'm getting word out as fast as I can."

"Oh, thank you for telling me. I'll give your friends a discount if they come in."

Nate shook his head. "There is no need to do that."

"But—"

"Most of these women can well afford your prices. Don't worry about that."

"All right, I'll charge them what I charge you."

Nate raised an eyebrow and grinned at her. "No. I have a feeling you are giving me a very good discount. You charge them the going rate."

Meagan sighed. She did give him a discount from what she normally charged. How could she not? He was the reason she'd been able to start her shop in the first place. "All right, I will."

"Good."

The waiter brought their meals out and served them. Once he was gone, Nate asked, "May I ask a blessing?"

"Of course you may," Meagan's mother said, and they bowed their heads while he did.

Meagan couldn't remember when she'd had a better time. Nate was attentive to her and her mother, and the conversation flowed smoothly. Of course, she gave the credit for that to her mother. They talked about the Crescent Hotel, which looked down over the town, and about what a beautiful addition it was to the landscape.

"It really is quite lovely on the inside. And the management is very dedicated to seeing that the guests are treated like royalty," Meagan's mother said.

"The opening gala is coming up soon. I'm sure it will be very lavish," Nate said.

"Oh, it will be. They were planning it before I left."

Meagan could only imagine what a gala at the hotel would be like. She'd heard it was by invitation only and was sure that only the richest and most influential people in town were invited—which certainly didn't include her.

That Nate knew many people in town became obvious as they enjoyed their meal, because several diners came up to their table and spoke to him. He was diligent in introducing them—never failing to mention her dressmaking shop.

A nice-looking couple stopped at the table, and Nate introduced them as Mr. and Mrs. Richardson.

"I've heard wonderful things about the quality of your work," Mrs. Richardson said. "I do need a few things for this spring and summer. Would it be possible for me to make an appointment to see you later today?"

"Of course. I should be back at the shop by three o'clock," Meagan said. "Could you come then?"

"I will be there. It was very nice to meet you and your mother," Mrs. Richardson said. "I'll call on you this afternoon, then."

The couple took their leave, and Meagan smiled at Nate. "Thank you. Again."

"You are very welcome. She's a very nice woman, and I'm sure she will be very pleased with the work you do for her. She'll also help spread the word."

Meagan hated to see the meal end. It was the first time she'd spent any time in Nate's company outside of the shop, besides at his bank and that one day at church. But that couldn't even be counted because he'd only been introducing them. This was different somehow.

They said their farewells outside the hotel, and Meagan spent the rest of the afternoon thinking about Nate and what a very nice man he was.

Over the first couple of weeks in April, Meagan ran into Nate at several other places, and she liked him more each time. First, they saw each other at the post office, where they spoke for several minutes. He asked about her mother and sisters and told her how much Natalie was looking forward to her next fitting. The next time she ran into him was at Martin's Dry Goods where she was picking up some thread and buttons and he was trying to select a doll for Natalie's birthday.

"Is her birthday coming up soon?" Meagan asked.

"It is two weeks from this Saturday. She is so excited. I hope she likes this doll. Do you think she will?" He held it up for her inspection. The lovely doll had hair the color of Natalie's and eyes the same shade as hers, too. She was dressed in the little girl's favorite color and the latest style.

"Oh, I think she will love it. It is beautiful."

"Good." He smiled and nodded. "I trust your judgment. I'll have it wrapped and sent to the house. My housekeeper, Mrs. Baker, will put it in my study."

He was through with his transaction before she was, but he waited for her to finish and walked out of the store with her. "Would you have time for a soda? There is a soda shop just across the street by the Perry House Hotel."

Meagan hesitated for only a moment. Her mother would be the first to encourage her to go. "I—I'd like that."

He put a hand on her elbow while they crossed the street and went into the shop. It was fairly quiet this time of day, and most of the seats at the counter were free, as were the small round tables. Nate led her to one of those and pulled out a chair for her. She'd been in the shop several times, but it had been awhile, and she'd never been in there with a gentleman.

That's exactly what Nate Brooks was—a very nice, gentle man. Yes, he was a banker, and she would always be thankful for all the ways he'd helped her and her family. But lately, she was seeing him as more than just a businessman. He was a wonderful father to Natalie, and he was easy to be around. *Much too easy to be around,* Meagan thought as he ordered their sodas and began telling her a funny story about Natalie.

She was laughing when their sodas were brought to the table.

Meagan felt more at ease around Nate each time she saw him, but this was the first time she'd actually had any real time with him alone. Conversation flowed easily between them until a clock in the shop chimed the hour.

Meagan realized they'd been there for over an hour. "Oh, I must be getting home. Mama will be getting worried about me."

Nate stood and pulled out her chair immediately. "I'll accompany you home and explain."

"Oh, no, that's not necessary. She will understand. But I'm sure she's beginning to wonder what has kept me so long."

"Well, I'd better let you go, then. Thank you for joining me this afternoon. I quite enjoyed it."

"You are welcome—so did I. Enjoy it, I mean. Thank you for treating me. Sodas are one of my very favorite things."

"I'll have to take you to the Crescent one of these days. I've been told that they have a wonderful soda shop there."

Meagan's heart felt all fluttery at the thought of him actually taking her to the Crescent. As they left the shop and she started home, however, she told herself it was time to quit daydreaming. Nate Brooks was a wonderful man, but they weren't in the same social circles, and nice as he was to her, it didn't mean that he was interested in her in any way other than seeing that her business was a success. *I need to remember that. Just because I find myself dreaming about him day and night doesn't mean he's dreaming about me. . . .*

&

Nate went back to the bank for an hour before going home. He'd enjoyed the afternoon even more than the lunch he'd had with Meagan and her mother. He wished that Meagan had let him see her home. He hadn't wanted the afternoon to end. It was always that way when he was with her.

From his observations, most of the women in his social circle visited with each other, entertained each other, and gossiped about each other. At times, he just wanted to leave the room. . .and often did. Meagan was so very different from them. It was refreshing just to be near her.

She was working to help her family, to keep her mother from working outside the home, and to give them all a future. He ventured to guess that none of the women he knew would handle the death of a parent and all the changes Meagan's family had gone through since then with such grace. He admired her greatly, and he hoped that by seeing him outside of the bank or her shop, she would get to know him better.

He thought back over the afternoon as he had his runabout brought around and headed home. He really cared about Meagan Snow. She was the first woman since his Rose that had touched his heart. He hoped she might begin to feel the same way about him.

He traveled up Spring Street to his home and prayed as the sun set behind the hill. *Thank You, Lord, for allowing me to run into Meagan the way I have been lately. I pray that if it be Your will, she will see me as a man who would like to court her. And I pray that You help me find a way to ask her if she will allow me to. In Jesus' name I pray. Amen.*

eight

"Aunt Abby and Grandmother, when are you going to visit Miss Meg's shop and have her make something for you?" Natalie asked at Sunday dinner the next week. "She makes such lovely things, and she showed me a ball gown she's making for someone. It is so beautiful."

"I am beginning to hear very good things about her," Abigail's mother said, ladling gravy over the potatoes on the plate she was serving to Nate. "I'm thinking of asking her to make me a new summer walking dress."

Inside, Abigail fumed, but she tried not to show it. As if she didn't hear enough about Meagan Snow from Natalie, now she was beginning to hear it from some of her friends *and* her mother. By all accounts the woman was a very good dressmaker—obviously word was getting around if her mother was thinking of doing business with her—but Abigail was sick of hearing her name.

"You should, Grandmother. She is making me one."

It seemed that Natalie was a one-woman advertising agency for that Snow woman's shop. *One would think she was being paid*, Abigail thought.

"I ran into Meagan and her mother having lunch the other day, and the Richardsons were there, too. Myla made an appointment to go see her." Nate's comment added to her irritation.

"Yes. Myla is having Miss Snow make her a new tea gown and a walking dress."

Abigail didn't much care—she just didn't like Natalie talking about her all the time, and she especially didn't like the fact that her niece saw so much of the woman. Suddenly, Abigail realized that if Natalie was going for fittings, unless the housekeeper was taking her, Nate was seeing an awful lot of Miss Snow, too.

"Does Mrs. Baker take Natalie to be fitted?"

"No." Natalie answered the question that had been directed to Nate. "Papa takes me."

"Oh, well, I know how busy you are, Nate. I'll be glad to take Natalie in for her fittings."

"Thank you, Abigail, but that won't be necessary. Miss Snow is very good about scheduling the fittings for when it is convenient for me."

"I see." And she didn't like what she was thinking. Not one bit.

"That's very nice of her," Abigail's mother said, handing Abigail her plate. "I've heard she is just a lovely woman."

Abigail made up her mind right then and there that it was time for her to get to know Miss Snow. And she would start tomorrow.

੨੦

Meagan couldn't be much happier with the way her business was growing. Mrs. Richardson had ordered several things from her, and through her word of mouth, two of her friends had come in and ordered new afternoon dresses. Occasionally, someone would see the sign outside and come in.

She was just finishing up the trim on a dinner dress she'd made for Mrs. Sinclair, one of the ladies who had come in the day of her opening, when she looked out the window and saw a woman approaching the shop. She came up the steps and around to the door. Meagan had a sinking feeling as she got up to greet her.

Abigail Connors swept into the shop as if she'd been coming for years. Meagan would know her anywhere. She saw her each Sunday, sitting on the same pew that Nate and Natalie used. . . often next to Nate. That she had a proprietary air toward Nate and Natalie was a big understatement. Now, here she was, in the one place Meagan had begun to weave dreams about herself and Nate.

Meagan forced a smile to her lips and held out her hand. "Good afternoon, Miss Connors. How nice to see you. How may I help you?"

"Thank you." The expression on the woman's face didn't match the tone of her voice at all. "How do you know who I am?"

"I've seen you at church with Mr. Brooks and Natalie. I've been doing some sewing for her."

"Ah, yes. I know," she said in a dismissive tone. "I've been hearing about your work. I'd like to see some samples of it if you have any to show me. I might decide to place an order with you if I like what I see."

Meagan could feel her face turn hot with indignation. How dare the woman take that tone with her? For a moment, Meagan thought she'd actually spoken aloud, and oh, how she wanted to. Instead, she silently prayed, asking for help not to lose her temper. This woman was Natalie's aunt and the daughter of the man who owned the bank that gave her the money to start this business. She could not afford to make her angry.

"I'd be glad to show you some of my work." She opened the wardrobe she and her mother had decided to put in the shop for just that reason. They used it to store some of the things Meagan had made for herself and other family members, rotating them with other outfits.

"Are you interested in anything in particular? An afternoon dress? Dinner dress?"

"Just show me what you have," Abigail said, pulling off the gloves that matched her afternoon dress of blue taffeta trimmed in gold. Meagan knew it was of the very latest style and fabric.

Thankful that she could show Abigail several things that were of just as good quality as what she was wearing and in the latest styles, as well, she pulled out an afternoon dress to show her. It was made of red- and white-striped serge with matching red trim at the neck and wrists. A solid red overskirt gathered up and draped to the side.

Abigail turned it this way and that, looking closely at the stitching. "This is very nice," she said. "What else do you have?"

Meagan showed one of her morning dresses and a walking dress that belonged to her mother. She also pulled out a dinner dress and a Sunday dress. Abigail went over each one as if she were buying them for herself or perhaps, given the way she was inspecting each one, the Queen of England! Meagan had never had her work scrutinized quite so thoroughly.

When she'd hung them all back, she turned to Abigail. "I hope you are satisfied that I do my best on each outfit I make, Miss Connors?"

Abigail rewarded her with a very slight nod. If Meagan had blinked, she would have missed it.

"You do fine work, Miss Snow. I can see why I've been hearing good reports about your skill as a dressmaker and why Nate keeps telling me to let all of my friends know about the shop."

Meagan's heart warmed at the thought that Nate was

trying to send more business to her.

"I would like to have a new dinner dress. Do you have some fashion plates available for me to look at?"

"Certainly." She motioned to the settee in front of the fireplace. "Please, make yourself comfortable. I just received the latest *Harpers Bazaar* and there are some lovely plates in it."

She handed the magazine to Abigail and then reached for another. "And here is the latest *Godey's* that I have. I'm sure we can find something in these."

As it was teatime and her mother always insisted that she stop working and take a brief break in the afternoon, Meagan wasn't surprised to see her enter the shop with a loaded tea tray. She'd taken to bringing in extra, just in case Meagan was with a customer, and she had never been so glad to see her mother as now.

"Mama, thank you. I didn't realize it was teatime already. Miss Connors, would you like a cup of tea and a tea cake?"

Abigail looked up from the magazine. "I—yes, I suppose I would."

"You do remember my mother from church, don't you?"

"No, I'm afraid I don't," Abigail said quite bluntly.

"There's no reason you should, Miss Connors," Meagan's mother said. "We only met that one time."

Meagan wanted to shout that there was every reason to remember her sweet mother, but she kept to the manners she'd been raised with and said nothing. Nevertheless, she certainly wasn't going to let her mother serve the woman.

"How would you like your tea? With cream and sugar?"

Abigail had gone back to perusing the magazine and didn't look up. "Yes, that will be fine."

"Would you like a tea cake?" Meagan asked. She could feel her eyebrow rise.

"No. Just tea."

Meagan looked at her mother and found her with a smile on her face and a twinkle in her eye as she fixed the cup of tea. Meagan sighed inwardly and smiled back as she took the cup of tea and set it down beside Abigail. "There you are."

The woman looked up from the magazine once more. "Yes, well, thank you."

"You are welcome. Have you seen anything you like?" Meagan took a sip of her own tea.

"Yes, in fact, I have." Abigail showed Meagan a fashion plate picturing a beautiful dinner dress in peacock blue satin trimmed in black Chantilly lace.

"That is lovely."

"Can you make something like that for me?"

"Of course. Would you want it in the same fabric? Or if not, I have several samples of other colors and different fabrics you may choose from."

"Let me look at those."

Never had Meagan dealt with a ruder woman. She wanted nothing more than to tell her so, but she couldn't. Instead, she sighed as she went to get her samples. Her mother just shook her head and left the room.

By the time Abigail left, Meagan had shown her every bolt and sample of fabric in the shop. After much deliberation, she finally decided that the design of the fashion plate would look better on her if it was made of a red-striped silk and black lace. Although Meagan thought it might be a little daring, she wasn't about to argue with the woman's choice.

"When can you start on it?" Abigail asked.

"I'll have to order the fabric and trim, but it shouldn't take more than a couple of weeks to come in. I can start on it then. I will need to take your measurements, though."

"Oh, yes. Can you do that now?"

"Certainly."

"It won't take long, will it? I'm having dinner with Nate and Natalie, and I don't want to be late."

Meagan's heart gave a sudden little twist. She didn't much like the idea of Nate having dinner with this woman—even if they were related by marriage. "It won't take long at all. You may use the screen behind you to remove your dress. Just let me know when you are ready."

When Abigail called, Meagan made quick work of getting her measurements. She wrote them down carefully in the notebook she kept for such purposes. "That will do it. I'll make note of these with your order. I'd like to make a muslin pattern and fit it to you. Can you come for a fitting a week from now?"

"I should be able to," Abigail said from behind the screen. "If not, I'll let you know."

"I'll give you an appointment card with the time before you leave."

She couldn't leave too soon for Meagan. When Abigail dressed and was ready to go, she took the card from Meagan and walked out the door without a word. Meagan released a huge sigh of relief. The very last thing she wanted was to sew for that woman, but there was absolutely no way to get out of it.

She locked the shop door and pulled down the shade that said CLOSED on the other side before gathering the teacups and tray and heading to the kitchen to see her mother. She set the tray down and dropped into a chair at the table.

Her mother turned from shaping the bread she was making for supper. "Her majesty has taken her leave, has she?"

"Finally. Oh, Mama! I do dread having to try to please her.

I've a feeling there will be no way I can do it."

"Just do the best you can, dear. It's all you can do."

"But what if she hates my work for her and spreads a bad word about me?"

"Her papa owns the bank that gave us the loan. She's not going to risk causing him to lose money by hurting your business, dear," her mother assured her.

"Surely she wouldn't." Meagan got up to heat water for a cup of fresh tea.

"You needn't worry anyway, dear. You are an excellent seamstress. She won't find anything to complain about."

"Oh, I hope you are right, Mama. She is one of the rudest women I've ever dealt with! I'm sure she was taught better."

"I certainly hope so." Her mother chuckled and shook her head. "Evidently she didn't learn it very well."

Meagan's sisters burst in from school just then, and the talk turned to their day. It seemed there was a new boy at school, and Becca kept teasing Sarah about him. From the color flooding her sister's cheeks, Meagan had a feeling that she might have taken a liking to him. She visited with the girls for a while and then went to finish trimming the dinner dress she'd been working on when Abigail came in. Her thoughts wandered as she hand stitched the trim around the bodice. Could it be possible that Nate had sent Abigail to check on her? No! He came in with Natalie often enough to know how her business was going. Besides, he wouldn't do that. Perhaps it was just because she wanted to find out herself how Meagan did business. Or perhaps it was because she wanted to make it very clear to Meagan that she had claim to Natalie and Nate....

nine

It seemed to Nate that he only saw Meagan when he took Natalie in for a fitting or briefly at church—although he never had a chance to speak to her there. Abigail saw to that. She seemed to be at his shoulder, slipping her hand through his arm as soon as the service was over. She always had something "important" to tell him or someone to introduce him to. By the time he got free, Meagan and her family had already left.

He was beginning to feel frustrated with the whole situation. He hadn't run into Meagan since the day he treated her to a soda, and just seeing her in the shop wasn't enough for him. She seemed to be in his thoughts often during the day, and he'd even begun to dream about her. He wanted to spend more time with her, but he wasn't sure how she might feel about that.

When Nate took Natalie in for a fitting of her new spring jacket the day before her birthday, Meagan seemed glad to see them. Her mother had made a special supper for Natalie, including her favorite cake. She would have a family celebration the next day, but Nate had a feeling that this was the one Natalie would enjoy most.

Before her mother served the cake, Meagan presented Natalie with a new reticule to match the jacket she'd just finished. Her mother and sisters had small gifts for her, too. Nate had never seen his daughter so happy and excited.

"Oh, thank you so much!" Natalie said. "I love it all. I'm having a party at my aunt Abby's tomorrow evening, but I know it's not going to be as nice as this."

"Oh, I'm sure it will be," Meagan assured her. "We just didn't want your birthday to come without giving you a little celebration."

"Thank you," Natalie said again. "I can't wait to show Grandmother and Aunt Abby my gifts!"

Nate heard Meagan's quick intake of breath, as if she were about to say something, but when he looked at her, she just gave a little shake of her head and began to hand out the cake.

Something about her seemed different though, and he wasn't sure what it was. When he and Natalie got ready to leave, it was even more apparent that something was different. While her attitude toward his daughter was still warm, he sensed a certain coolness toward him. Nate wanted to ask if something was wrong, but with his daughter and Meagan's family right there, he didn't feel it was the right time.

"Thank you all for helping to make Natalie's birthday so special."

"Yes, thank you!" Natalie said. "It was ever so much fun! And I love my gifts. Thank you so very much!"

"We were happy to be able to celebrate with you," Mrs. Snow said.

"And I love my new coat, Miss Meg. It is just like I pictured it, only better. And thank you again for my reticule!"

Meagan's smile for his daughter was completely genuine, of that Nate had no doubt.

"I'm glad you are happy with it. It was a joy to make it for you." She bent down and gave Natalie a hug. "I hope you have a happy day tomorrow."

As Nate watched the expression on his daughter's face when she hugged Meagan back, he knew he wasn't the only one who cared for Meagan Snow.

ﾟ

Meagan blew the hair off her forehead as soon as the door closed on Nate and Natalie.

"Come have a cup of tea, dear," her mother said. "I can tell you are upset."

Meagan let out a ragged sigh and followed her mother to the kitchen where Becca and Sarah were cleaning up. She didn't know who she was trying to convince when she said, "I have no right to be upset, Mama."

"That may be so, but you are. What is wrong?"

"It was the mention of Abigail Connors," Meagan said, dropping into a chair at the table. "I do not see how she could be related in any way to Natalie. That child is so sweet and her aunt is. . .a. . .a viper!"

"Now, Meagan, dear, that's a bit strong, don't you think?" Her mother made a cup of tea and handed it to Meagan, then poured herself one and joined her at the table.

"I suppose it might be. But she is just so condescending and rude. And she acts as if she owns Natalie and Mr. Brooks. She never fails to point out how often she spends time with them and all they do together, or how she's always been there for the two of them ever since her sister died in the fire." Meagan sighed and began to rub her temple. "When Natalie tells Abigail about her party here and what we gave her. . .well, I don't think she's going to be happy. She isn't going to like the fact that we celebrated Natalie's birthday here at all."

"Ahh, I believe I'm beginning to see."

Meagan shook her head. "No, Mama. I know my place. Mr. Brooks will not be courting me—I don't belong in his social circle. Abigail Connors has a way of making me realize that. Besides, I—"

"Meagan Snow, I'll not have you talking like that. You are

just as good as that Connors woman and anyone in her circle. When he worked for the railroad, your papa was just as well thought of as Mr. Connors is. Don't you ever think you have to belong in a certain circle before you are good enough for anyone. The only circle you need worry about is the one that God is at the center of."

"I know, Mama. I'm sorry. I didn't mean to upset you."

"Just don't talk like that again. Nate Brooks would be a very lucky man indeed if you cared for him."

Meagan took a sip of her tea, afraid that if she looked her mother in the eye, she'd be able to see that Meagan already did care for Nate—much too much for her own good.

ॐ

Meagan couldn't deny that she'd been cool toward Nate after Natalie's birthday celebration. She didn't mean to be. She felt badly about it, yet events of the weekend had her feeling even more upset.

On Sunday, Nate had somehow managed to get out of his pew and head back toward her and her family before Abigail could grab him. She was, however, right behind him.

Meagan's first instinct was to flee, but her mother put a constraining hand on her shoulder, and she realized she couldn't be that rude.

"Good morning, Mrs. Snow, Meagan, Becca, and Sarah," Nate said with a smile.

Her family greeted him the same way they always did.

His eyes were on her, however, and as Abigail was sidling up to him, all Meagan could muster was a weak smile and a quiet, "Good morning."

"I just wanted to thank you again—"

"Oh, dear Meagan," Abigail interrupted Nate, "the jacket you made our Natalie is just beautiful. I can't wait to have the first fitting of the dress you are making me!"

"Thank you," was all Meagan managed to say.

Nate looked irritated as he continued, "I was thanking you for helping to make Natalie's birthday even more special than usual."

The subject of the conversation came running up the aisle. "Miss Meg, everyone loves my jacket! I've been telling everyone who asks that it was you who made it!"

Meagan couldn't help but smile at the child's sweetness. "Why, thank you, Natalie. That is very nice of you."

"Well, yes, it was, dear," Abigail said, pulling Natalie close to her side. "We're getting out the word as fast as we can. But now we must leave. Mama and Papa will be wondering what is keeping us today."

Nate let out an audible sigh but nodded. "I suppose we should be going. I hope you have a very nice day, ladies."

"Thank you," Meagan's mother said. "You have a wonderful one, too."

Abigail put her hand on Nate's arm and turned to Meagan. "Good-bye. I'll be in for my fitting this week."

All Meagan could do was nod at the woman and try to smile.

It certainly wasn't a great afternoon for her. She was out of sorts the rest of the day and even into the next. With Abigail and some of her friends as her clients now, Meagan was reminded almost daily that Nate's social life wasn't the kind she led. Her life was filled with family, work, and church. And while she wished she were going to the Crescent's Grand Opening Gala, it wasn't the kind of thing she would want to do often. Yet from what she heard from Abigail and some of her friends, their lives seemed filled with parties and elegant dinners and—

She had to chuckle. It was all those things that would keep her in business. She was fortunate to be able to sew for the ladies who attended all of those social gatherings. They were the ones who paid more for their outfits and would get her business on sound financial footing. One day, she'd be able to pay off the bank loan. Then, perhaps she could ask Miss Abigail Connors to find someone else to sew for her.

Meagan sighed and shook her head. No. Not even then. She still couldn't risk making Abigail angry. The woman would waste no time trying to get her friends and acquaintances to go elsewhere, too. Meagan was just going to have to put up with Abigail and be thankful for the business she might help bring in. Most importantly, she needed to pray for the Lord to give her patience and a proper attitude toward Abigail.

She was also bothered by how she had been treating Nate recently. It wasn't his fault she didn't like his sister-in-law, and she shouldn't be letting those feelings have anything to do with how she treated Nate. He probably thought she was awful. Perhaps he even regretted giving her the loan—

The bell over the shop door rang, and Meagan looked up to see the man in her thoughts come inside. "Nate. . .is something wrong? I don't think Natalie is due for a fitting."

But Natalie wasn't with him, and she felt silly for mentioning it.

He smiled. "Everything is fine. . .at least with me. I was wondering the same about you. You've seemed a little. . .as if something is bothering you the last few times I've seen you, and I wanted to make sure that I haven't offended you in some way."

She jumped up from her sewing machine and assured him, "Oh, no, Nate. You haven't offended me at all."

"I'm glad. I've wanted to ask you something for several weeks now."

"Oh? What is it?" Her heartbeat sped up.

"Well, you know the Grand Opening Gala at the Crescent is being held next month?"

"Yes, I know." She held her breath, waiting to hear what he was going to say next.

"I was wondering. . .would you accompany me to it?"

For a moment, Meagan couldn't breathe. He was asking her to the biggest event so far in the season. "I—I—"

"I know it is late notice, with it being only three weeks away, and I apologize for that. If you already have an escort, I understand. But if not, I would be honored if you would be my guest."

Meagan felt as if her heart were going to pound right out of her chest. She had assumed he'd be taking Abigail and had never thought that he might ask her. . .although she couldn't deny that she'd dreamed about it several times. And much as she wanted to go, she felt she should say no—

"I would really like you to go with me, Meagan. I never feel quite comfortable at these things, yet I'm expected to go to them. I think it would be so much easier if you were there with me."

"Oh, I. . ." That he felt uncomfortable at something like that touched her. "But I can't dance. I don't know how."

"It doesn't matter. We don't have to dance." He tilted his head and grinned at her. "Please?"

Her heart turned to mush. There was just no way she could bring herself to say no. "I would love to go with you, Nate."

ten

Dinner was almost over before Abigail remembered to ask what time Nate would be picking her up for the gala the next week.

"I'm not escorting you, Abigail," Nate said.

"You aren't escorting me? Why, you always. . ." What was he thinking?

"No, Abigail, I don't," Nate said. "We are usually at the same gatherings, but I rarely escort you to them."

"Well, I assumed you would be taking me to this. It's the biggest event of the year! Why aren't you going?"

"I am going. I'm sorry, Abigail, but I've already invited someone else."

"Who?" She could feel a severe headache coming on. This couldn't be happening. How was she going to find an escort at this late date? It was only a week until the gala.

"I invited Miss Snow to accompany me."

"Meagan Snow? The *seamstress*?"

"She is the owner of a dressmaking shop. . .not just a seamstress, Abigail."

Abigail could feel the color rushing to her face. "Well, whatever she is—"

"Abigail, dear," her mother interrupted, nodding her head in Natalie's direction. "Now is not the time to discuss this."

Natalie's eyes were big and round, and she looked as if she were about to cry. Abigail took a deep breath and tried to tamp down her temper as she knew her parents expected.

She sighed and nodded. "Very well."

If it hadn't been for her parents stepping in, total silence would have reigned at the table. Abigail didn't know what the conversation was about, and she let it flow around her. All she could think of was that Nate had chosen Meagan Snow over her.

The more she thought about it, the angrier she became. How dare Nate not take her? What was he thinking? He should have known she expected him to accompany her. This was the biggest event in Eureka Springs this season, and Nate was aware that she wasn't being courted by anyone. Of course, it wasn't for lack of trying on several of her men friends' parts—particularly Robert Ackerman. He'd made no secret that he was very interested in her. The only man she'd ever been interested in, however, was Nate. Now, instead of taking her to the gala, he was taking a mere seamstress. Why? Perhaps it was to help her business by introducing her to the wealthy women in town. But that was already happening. No. Much as she hated the very thought, Abigail was afraid it was simply because he cared about Meagan Snow and wanted her to go with him. That was not going to do. It just wasn't going to do at all.

❧

Nate knew he would remember the Crescent opening for the rest of his life. Meagan was more than lovely in her porcelain blue silk ball gown. Her hair was dressed in a more elaborate style than usual, and her eyes were bright and shining. He was sure it was just in excitement about the gala, and not necessarily because she was going with him, but he was glad he was taking her.

He'd rented a carriage to take them in style, and it wasn't dark yet when they started up the hill to Prospect Avenue where the Crescent, built out of limestone, appeared to be almost castlelike, looking down over its village below. When the driver stopped at the entrance to the Crescent, attendants helped Meagan out of the carriage before Nate had a chance to.

He pulled her hand through his arm, however, and led her up entrance steps into the huge foyer where people were arriving and meeting up with others they knew. He began to introduce her to his friends and some of the bank's customers but was pleased that she recognized other people whom she felt comfortable around, too.

Her neighbors Mr. and Mrs. Morrison were attending. Mrs. Morrison was wearing the ball gown that Meagan had made for her, and she looked lovely. "I've had so many compliments on my gown, and I'm taking the opportunity to tell everyone who asks about your shop, dear. Now that I know you are here, I can send them your way," Mrs. Morrison said.

"Oh, thank you!"

They made their way to the Grand Ballroom. Tables had been set up around the huge room, and they found one that had an opening for Nate and Meagan and the Morrisons. Nate knew several others at the table and made introductions.

It was very relaxing to be at a different table than the one Abigail and her friends were at. He'd spotted her across the room, and if her expression was anything to go by—and it usually was—she still wasn't happy with him. He didn't want to upset her, but she'd become much too possessive of him, and it was time she realized he wasn't her property. He turned his attention to Meagan and the people at his table.

Mr. Powell Clayton, the president of the railway and one of the town's outstanding citizens with the Eureka Springs Improvement Company and various other endeavors, stopped by the table with his wife. Nate was somewhat surprised when Mr. Clayton began talking to Meagan about her father.

"He was a good railroad man, your papa," Mr. Clayton said. "We've missed him greatly. I was honored to have known him."

Nate saw tears well up in Meagan's eyes, but she got them under control and smiled. "Thank you. That means so much to me."

"I've heard that you have gone into business for yourself?"

"Yes, sir, I am a seamstress and—"

"She is not just a seamstress," Mrs. Morrison said. "She also designs some of her creations. She is a dressmaker whose name will always mean quality workmanship and exquisite design."

Nate smiled and added his opinion, even though it wasn't needed. "Miss Snow has quite a talent. I don't think there is anything she can't make. And whether her own design or from a fashion plate, the end result is always better than expected."

"I take it you made the gown you have on?" Mrs. Clayton asked.

"She made mine, also. It is one of her original designs," Mrs. Morrison said before Meagan could answer.

"You made both of them?"

"Yes, ma'am, I did," Meagan answered modestly.

"I'll be in to see you next week."

"I'd love that. The dress you have on is very lovely."

"Yes, well, it's seen its best day. I think it is time I have a new ball gown, don't you, Powell, dear?"

"Anything you want to have Miss Snow make for you is fine with me, dear."

One of the other men at the table laughed. "Spoken like a smart husband."

"I take it I'll get the same answer if I order something from Miss Snow?" his wife asked.

"Of course you will," he answered.

More laughter followed the Claytons as they rushed to their table for the first course of oysters in half shells, which was just arriving. Nate could see that Meagan was having a good time, and he let himself relax and enjoy the evening, too.

Mock turtle soup arrived next, followed by lobster farci and then fillet of beef with mushroom sauce. Nate lost count of the side dishes but enjoyed the lemon pie.

Once they finished the meal, Reverend McElwee gave the invocation and then Mr. Clayton took to the podium to introduce the guest of honor, the Honorable James G. Blaine, the Republican presidential nominee of 1884. After he spoke, there would be a brief break while the tables were cleared, and then the popular Harry Barton and his orchestra would begin the night's entertainment.

Nate took that opportunity to take Meagan around and introduce her to some of the people he knew. First, they went to a table across the room, and he introduced her to Mr. and Mrs. Connors. They were very gracious to her.

"I've been hearing good things about the dress shop you've opened, Miss Snow. Connors Bank is glad to have had the chance to be a part of it."

"Thank you, sir. I can't thank you enough for giving me the opportunity to go into business."

"The credit isn't mine. Nate saw the possibilities. He's also a great asset to Connors Bank. I wish you much success."

"Thank you," Meagan said once more before Nate led her away.

"I have to do this or I'll not have any friends left," he said as he led her over to the table where Abigail and his friends sat. As he introduced Meagan, he realized that most of the people he socialized with were Abigail's friends. . .and he wasn't all that fond of most of them.

But they were all very nice to Meagan, and for that he was grateful. He would have hated for them to snub her or treat her with disdain because of Abigail's attitude.

Abigail spoke but was very cool. Meagan didn't seem to let it bother her. She was polite to her and the others, and when several of the women asked about her shop, he knew that fashion had triumphed over loyalty to Abigail.

As they were on their way back to their table, Meagan excused herself to go to the ladies' room.

It was then that Abigail cornered him.

"Why didn't you sit at our table tonight, Nate? Were you embarrassed by your companion?"

"Not at all! I thought she might be more comfortable with people she knew. If I were embarrassed, I wouldn't have introduced her to everyone. They seem to like her."

"Yes, well I'm sure she'll fit right in," Abigail said a bit sarcastically. "I still can't understand why you brought her."

"You don't have to, Abigail."

"Well! You don't have to be rude!"

Nate sighed. "Abigail, I'm sorry you are upset with me. I'm not trying to be rude. But who I choose to bring is really none of your business."

"I'm family, Nate."

"That doesn't mean you have to approve of whom I choose to keep company with."

Saying nothing, Abigail swept her skirts around and flounced off in a huff in the direction of the ladies' room. Nate had a feeling she wanted to stomp her feet. He could only hope that Meagan wasn't still there.

Lately Abigail had an edge to her that he didn't like. He wasn't sure she was a good influence on his daughter, either.

Abigail had become quite snobbish through the years. Or had she always been that way? Perhaps he should think about limiting the time Natalie spent with her aunt.

ᐱ

Meagan had never had an evening such as this one. She felt like a princess. She'd met many of Eureka Springs's most prominent citizens and was especially impressed with Mr. and Mrs. Connors and the Claytons. She'd been stopped on the way to the ladies' room by first one lady and then another to ask if she was the one who made Mrs. Morrison's gown.

By the time she got to the ladies' room and to the mirror, she found there was no need to pinch her cheeks to put a little color to them. Her face was flushed with the sheer excitement of the evening. She'd had two women ask if they could come in on Monday, and another asked the same for Tuesday.

She was just turning to leave when Abigail Connors entered the room. Meagan's heart seemed to stop beating at the look in the woman's eyes. She nodded and tried to smile, but Miss Connors was not smiling. She barely nodded as she swept past Meagan. That she was angry was obvious, and Meagan was sure the fact that she'd come with Nate was the reason. She was thankful other women were milling around—she felt that might be the only reason Abigail hadn't told her just what she thought of her being here with Nate.

Meagan rushed back to her table as fast as possible. She wanted to get as far away from Abigail Connors as she could.

Nate looked at her closely when she got back to their table, but she smiled and took her seat without mentioning Abigail. She hoped that she hadn't made life harder for Nate by coming with him. Even if he never asked her anywhere else, she would be thankful to him for this evening.

The orchestra added to the enchantment of the evening, and Meagan began to tap her foot in time to the music.

"Would you like to learn to dance?" Nate leaned near and asked. "I could teach you a few steps."

At the very thought of being held in Nate's arms, Meagan's heart began to beat so fast it was hard to speak. All she could manage was, "You could?"

"Certainly. I would love to teach you."

"I would love to learn," Meagan admitted. She looked around the room at the couples who seemed to be floating across the floor. "But not here in front of everyone." She shook her head. "Maybe another time?"

Nate scooted back his chair and stood. "Perhaps we can get some air, then." He pulled out her chair. "Come with me."

Meagan felt his hand at her elbow as he steered her toward one of the double doors leading out of the ballroom. Then he led her down the stairs to an outside terrace where several other couples had decided to get some fresh air, too. They could still hear the orchestra in the quiet of the evening.

"Oh, it's lovely here," Meagan said. The fragrance of blooming flowers lent sweetness to the night air, and the lights from residences up and down the hillside made her realize just how far up they were.

"It is, isn't it? Not near as lovely as you, though," Nate said.

Meagan caught her breath at his words. She wasn't sure what to say, except, "Thank you."

Following a lull in the music, the orchestra began to play again, and Nate turned to her. "A waltz. Perfect. Won't you let me show you some steps now?"

"I—yes, please," Meagan said. How thoughtful of him to get her away from any chance of ridicule for her clumsiness.

He bowed and slipped his right arm around her waist,

holding out his left hand for hers. Meagan slipped her hand into his, and he drew her nearer. "One, two, three," Nate began to count as he showed her the steps. "One, two, three." The pressure from his hand told her when to turn. "One, two, three. You're getting it. One, two, three."

Meagan found it quite easy to follow his lead, the slight pressure on her back telling her when and in what direction he wanted her to turn. She lost track of time and was quite disappointed when the music ended. Nate sighed and kept his arm around her for a moment before letting her go. "You are an excellent student. Would you like to go in and dance around the ballroom floor now?"

"Oh. . .I'm not sure I'm ready for that—to dance in front of everyone. But thank you for the lesson. I enjoyed—"

"Another waltz," Nate interrupted as the music began again. "Let me have one more dance out here, then." He looked down into her eyes and smiled. Reaching out and tucking an errant curl behind her ear, he whispered, "Please."

He was asking her to do the very thing she wanted—to step into his arms again. "All right."

Nate's arm encircled her once more and pulled her close. Meagan's heart began to pound in time to the music as they floated around the limestone terrace. She wished the evening would never come to an end.

eleven

Nate hated to see the evening end—he hated to part company with Meagan. Even Abigail's bad mood hadn't put a damper on his evening. All he need do was look at Meagan, and all thoughts of Abigail's anger disappeared.

"Oh, what a lovely evening," Meagan said as he helped her into the carriage.

It was beautiful. The moon was huge, and the stars bright and numerous. The air was balmy and fragrant.

"It is, isn't it?" Nate took his place beside her and motioned for the driver to take off. "Lovely as it is, though, the night sky really doesn't compare to how you look tonight, Meagan," he complimented her once more.

"Oh, why. . .thank you, Nate."

The way she ducked her head, he had a feeling she was blushing as she often did when he paid her a compliment. If so, he wished he could see the captivating color flood her cheeks. "You're welcome. I thank you for accompanying me this evening, Meagan. And thank you for letting me teach you to dance the waltz. I can't remember when I've had a better time."

"It was a wonderful evening. I've never been anywhere as nice as the Crescent before. Obviously, I'd never danced before tonight. Thank you for teaching me and for asking me to accompany you, Nate."

"Please—quit thanking me. I was honored to be your escort." *More than honored.* He was also proud just to be seen with her. More than one man had come up to him and asked who she was while she was in the ladies' room. The whole evening had been one to remember, but the highlight for him was waltzing with Meagan on the terrace. No. He would never forget this night.

"Everyone looked so elegant, and oh, the food was so delicious."

Nate chuckled. "It was very good. They hired an excellent chef." He loved Meagan's fresh perspective on the evening. When the carriage stopped at her house, Nate helped her down and asked the driver to wait for him. He walked her to the door and admitted, "I hate to see the evening end."

"Mama and the girls will be up, wanting a full account of the opening. Would you like to come in and have some lemonade? I'm sure Mama has some made."

"I would love some if you are sure your mother won't mind."

"She'll be happy to see you."

Meagan opened the door, and her mother must have been listening for the sound, because she came out of the kitchen, followed by Sarah and Becca.

"Mama, I asked Nate in for lemonade or something cool to drink, but he wants to make sure it's all right with you."

"Of course it is." Mrs. Snow smiled. "You are always welcome in this home, Nate. We've all been waiting to hear about the evening. Please, come on back to the kitchen."

Nate was beginning to feel at home in this kitchen. He loved it there. It was warm and welcoming, even when nothing was on the stove or in the oven.

Meagan looked beautiful as he held out a chair for her. She didn't look out of place at all sitting at their kitchen table in all her finery. Her sisters helped her mother, and soon he had a glass of lemonade sitting before him.

"Thank you," Nate said and took his first sip. "The last time I sat in a kitchen and drank lemonade, I was about Sarah's age. This takes me back to my mother's kitchen, Mrs. Snow. It's a good memory. Thank you."

"You're welcome, Nate."

As they all sat around the table, he and Meagan filled the others in on the Crescent gala. He mostly listened unless Meagan asked for his input.

She described the inside of the Crescent in detail, although her mother knew what it looked like from working there. But it hadn't been quite as dressed up then, she said. Meagan went on to describe the gowns some of the women had been wearing and how they'd sat at the same table as their neighbors, and she told them about meeting the Claytons.

It was while Meagan described the women and how lovely they all looked that Nate realized how very different she was from Abigail. Abigail would have been critical of each and every woman there and what she had on. It was what she and her friends always did, and then when one of them left the table or room, the others talked about that one. He often wondered how they could not recognize that they were all talking about each other.

Even if Meagan and her family didn't like someone, he didn't think they would talk about them that way. He'd never heard any of that when he was around them. Sitting in this kitchen with this family made him aware of the fact that he really hadn't been true to himself or his upbringing in the last few years.

When the clock struck the hour, he knew it was time to leave. He certainly didn't want to wear out his welcome. As Meagan and her family saw him to the door, Nate realized he had a lot to think about. Perhaps it was time he made some changes. He left the house that had become some kind of haven for him and headed home.

He was falling in love with Meagan Snow, but he wasn't sure she was even aware of how much he cared for her. Part of him was afraid to let her know, and the other couldn't wait to tell her how he felt. He wasn't sure the time was right. He prayed for the Lord to help him sort it all out and to be able to find a way to convince Meagan that he truly cared for her.

❧

Once Nate and that Snow woman left the gala, Abigail was no longer interested in staying. She insisted her escort take her home, although he wasn't happy about it. She didn't much care. All she wanted to do was get home. She wasn't in the mood to make small talk when all she could think of was Nate and the fact that he appeared to be very interested in Meagan Snow. That just wasn't going to do at all.

Millie helped her out of her gown and brought a pot of tea to her room as Abigail always expected. "Here you go, Miss Abigail. How was the gala? You looked so beautiful tonight— I'm sure it was an evening you'll never forget."

"No. I never will, Millie." Abigail couldn't hold her anger in any longer. "Actually, it was one of the worst nights of my life!"

"Oh, I'm so sorry. What happened?"

"Nate and that—"Abigail caught herself before she confided in her hired help. "I don't want to talk about it."

Millie nodded and poured a cup of tea for her. "I understand. Would you like anything else, ma'am?"

"No. You may retire for the night."

"Thank you, Miss Abigail. Good night."

Abigail sighed as her housekeeper left the room. She did like tea; it usually settled her nerves. Not tonight. She sipped from her cup as she looked out the window into the night.

She was too keyed up to stay still, and she felt like a caged tiger as she paced her room. *There must be something I can do to nip this little romance in the bud.* She couldn't just let Meagan Snow win Nate's heart!

Abigail had been biding her time ever since her sister, Rose, had died, hoping that one day Nate would realize how much she loved him. She'd resented Rose since the day Nate began to court her and even more once they'd had a child. Nevertheless, she loved her niece. That day of the fire was one she rarely let herself think about, but now she couldn't keep the memories back.

She'd stopped by to bring a present to three-year-old Natalie. When the fire broke out, there was confusion. She and Rose ran from one window to the next, trying to see where it was. When they found that the flames were jumping from one building to the other up the hillside, they knew they didn't have much time to salvage anything.

"Abigail, the fire will be here any moment. We must get Natalie to safety!" Rose handed the child to her. "I have to get the picture albums. I'll hurry!"

Rose started up the staircase. Hugging the child close, Abigail followed. "No, Rose. There isn't time! We need to go now."

"It won't take a minute. I must get the mementos that mean so much to us. Take Natalie to safety. I'll be right behind you."

"No, Rose, you must come now! The fire is almost here!" Abigail grabbed Rose's arm, but her sister pulled away, losing her balance. Abigail screamed as she watched her sister tumble from the landing to the bottom of the staircase. She rushed to help her, but Rose was badly hurt. By then the flames had reached the house.

"Get. . .Natalie to. . .safety," Rose whispered before she

passed out. Abigail grabbed the child and ran, intending to come back to help Rose, but when she turned back, the house was engulfed in flames. Nate showed up and rushed past her, trying to save his wife. But flames surged out of the house, and it was too late.

As she and Nate tried to comfort each other in those moments, hugging Natalie close, Abigail hated herself for the errant thought that came to mind. *Finally, Rose is out of the way.* Maybe now, Nate would make her his wife.

Abigail shook her head, trying to push away the guilt she'd felt that day. She had loved Nate long before he married her sister. And ever since Rose's death, Abigail had hoped that one day Nate would look at her and realize he loved her, too. Yet it had been four years since her sister died—four years of waiting and hoping.

It hadn't been terribly hard. Nate wasn't interested in anyone else. His life revolved around Natalie, and that was all right with Abigail. She loved her niece as if she were her own. Life hadn't been bad. She spent a great deal of it with Nate and Natalie, and she had been hopeful that he would finally see it was in Natalie's best interest for them to marry. Now time seemed to be running out, and she must do something. She hadn't waited all these years to let some new woman come in and take away the only man she'd ever loved. It just wasn't going to happen.

❧

After Nate left, the girls went upstairs to get ready for bed, and Meagan helped her mother clean up the kitchen. It was then that she told her about running into Abigail.

"She's not happy with me at all, Mama. I probably shouldn't have accepted Nate's invitation." She put up the last cup and leaned against the doorframe.

"She's not married to him, Meagan. He was free to ask any-one he wanted to accompany him to the gala. It was you he wanted to go with."

"I know. But she is one of my customers now—not to mention that her father owns the bank that gave us the loan."

"I doubt her father does business according to his daughter's moods, dear. Besides, Nate runs that bank. I don't think that Mr. Connors is that involved in the day-to-day managing of it anymore."

"But he—"

"Meagan, I'm sure he has Nate's welfare to consider also. After all, he's the father of Mr. Connors's granddaughter. He has her welfare to take into consideration, too."

"That's true. I just hope tonight doesn't cause problems for Nate. Will you help me out of this gown, Mama?"

"Of course I will. I'm ready to go up, too."

Meagan didn't bring up the subject of Nate again while her mother helped her out of the gown. She hung it in the wardrobe while Meagan changed into her gown and wrapper. "You looked lovely tonight, my Meagan. I'm sure there wasn't a woman there who looked any prettier than you did. I'm so glad you got to go."

"Thank you, Mama. Many women there looked more elegant than I did, but I had such a wonderful time. It's a night I'll never forget."

"I'm glad. Good night, dear."

"Good night, Mama."

After her mother left, Meagan read her Bible and said her prayers, but she still had a hard time getting to sleep. She was much too excited to settle down. She went downstairs and made herself a cup of tea, then took it back to her room and sat down in the chair beside her bed. It had been a night to remember. Nate had treated her as if she were the most special woman in the world, and for a while, she had felt as if she were. . .particularly when he'd held her in his arms and danced with her.

Then she remembered running into Abigail. Meagan took a sip of tea. She wasn't sure how to act when the woman came into the shop this next week for a fitting, but she couldn't worry about it now. What she must do was realize that she could never fit into Nate's social group. She had enjoyed the evening and knew it was a night she would never forget. But she was beginning to care too much for Nate Brooks, and there was no future in that. Oh, how he made her stomach flutter when she was around him.

Meagan sighed and took another sip of tea. Although she was glad she'd accepted his invitation, part of her wished she hadn't gone with him this evening. It was only going to make it harder to accept the fact that there was no future in giving her heart to him. There would only be heartache ahead. Abigail Connors had not liked it at all that Nate was with Meagan tonight. And even if he wasn't interested in Abigail, she was part of his daughter's family and could make life miserable for him.

No. For everyone's sake, she had to stop dreaming about a future with Nate. It was going to lead nowhere. She took one more sip of tea and then got on her knees.

"Dear Lord, You've been with me through all the heartaches in my life, and I know You will help me now. I'm afraid I'm falling in love with Nate Brooks, but I would never fit into his social circle. . .nor would I really want to. We live in two different worlds, and I don't see how they can ever merge. Please help me to accept that and quit thinking of him night and day. In Jesus' name, I pray. Amen."

twelve

Knowing that she needed to put Nate out of her mind and quit dreaming about him was one thing, but during the next few days, Meagan found doing it was quite another. She saw him and Natalie at church, but Abigail had a grip on his arm as soon as the service was over, and they were out the door before Meagan had a chance to even wave. Natalie wasn't coming in for a fitting until later in the week.

Abigail, however, would be in for a fitting on Wednesday afternoon. She brought her mother with her, and Meagan found that Mrs. Connors was nothing like her daughter. She was gracious and kind and had only good words to say.

"I've been meaning to come in and see about having you make me a few things. After I saw samples of your work at the gala, I didn't want to delay any longer, so I insisted Abigail bring me with her today."

"Thank you, Mrs. Connors. I have several magazines with the newest fashion plates. Would you like to look at them?"

"I'm not sure we have the time, Mother," Abigail said.

"Of course we do, dear. I can look at them while you are changing and having your fitting. If I need to make an appointment to come in by myself, I'll do that. But yes, Miss Snow, I would love to look at your magazines." She settled herself in the settee and took the magazines from Meagan.

"My mother will be in shortly with tea, Mrs. Connors. She always brings some in this time of day."

"That will be lovely, dear," the older woman said. "I'd enjoy a cup of tea."

"Very well, Mother." Abigail sighed in resignation as she went behind the screen to change into the dress Meagan was making for her.

While Meagan could tell Abigail wasn't very happy, she was quite relieved that Abigail's mother was with her. Meagan had been dreading this fitting ever since the evening of the gala. From Abigail's attitude, Meagan was fairly certain that if it hadn't been for Mrs. Connors's insistence, Abigail would have come by herself—probably to warn her away from Nate.

When her mother brought in the tea tray, Meagan introduced the two women and was very pleased that they seemed to like each other. She left her mother to serve tea to Mrs. Connors while she went to help Abigail with the hooks on her dress.

But even with both of their mothers in the room, Abigail managed to get in her barbs.

"How did you enjoy the gala?" Abigail asked.

"I enjoyed it very much."

"I thought it was very nice of Nate to introduce you to so many people. Of course, that's Nate. He's always looking after the bank's interests."

Meagan took a sharp intake of breath at Abigail's words. Was that why Nate had asked her to accompany him? It easily could have been. Her heart twisted at the very thought.

She didn't know what to say, so she said nothing. Still, Abigail didn't let up. For the rest of the time she was there, Abigail managed to let Meagan know that she had a prior claim to her brother-in-law. As she swept around the screen to show her mother the dinner gown Meagan had made her, she turned this way and that. "I think this will work for the dinner I'm hosting for Nate's birthday, don't you, Mother?"

She stood on the small platform Meagan had asked Mr. Adams to build for her to make it easier to pin hems. Abigail turned when Meagan asked her to, while she pinned the hem of the garment.

"It's beautiful, dear. It would work for any dinner you might host," her mother replied, watching her daughter turn slowly as Meagan pinned.

Once she was finished, Abigail slowly turned again, looking in the mirrors Meagan had set up in the shop. The red on red-striped silk did look wonderful on her, bringing out the blue in her eyes and her blond hair.

"I think I'll have you make me a new gown to wear to the opera, too, Miss Snow," Abigail said. "When Nate took me, although he told me I looked lovely in my blue silk, I realized I needed something new to add to my wardrobe for the upcoming season."

Meagan felt another twinge at the mention of Nate taking Abigail to the opera. Obviously, the woman was trying to let Meagan know that just because he'd taken her to the gala didn't mean that he was going to be escorting her anywhere else. Abigail was getting her message across quite well.

Making the woman another gown was the last thing Meagan wanted to do. She had been hoping that Abigail would satisfy whatever curiosity it was that brought her into the shop and have her make just this one dress and then leave Meagan alone. But it seemed she wasn't going to do that. And as she was the daughter of the man who owned the bank and her mother was sitting in the very same room, Meagan couldn't very well say no. "You are welcome to look over the new plates. I'm sure we can find something to please you."

"I've found a few I like already. I'll look them over again when I come for my next fitting."

"Well, I've already found a few things I love," Mrs. Connors said. "But I know my daughter is in a hurry, so I'll come back in to see you next week if you have a time available for me."

Meagan checked the appointment book she'd just begun to need. "Monday at two will work for me, if that is convenient for you."

"That will be fine."

"Miss Snow!" Abigail called from behind the screen. "Are you going to help me get out of this gown?"

"Of course," Meagan said, hurrying to do just that. Abigail Connors couldn't leave fast enough to please her.

"Abigail! Miss Snow was taking care of me."

"I'm sorry, Mother. But we do have to change before we meet Papa for dinner at the Crescent," Abigail said from behind the screen.

Meagan helped her out of the dress. "I should have this ready for you by Saturday. Would you like me to have it sent to your home, or do you want to pick it up and look over the plates again then?"

"You may have it sent to my home. Since I won't need to come in for another fitting now, I will find the plate I like and pick out the fabric before Mother and I leave. I want to look my best this season." She turned and looked Meagan in the eye and lowered her voice. "I plan on being Mrs. Nate Brooks by this time next year."

Meagan held up the dress Abigail had worn into the shop, thankful for the yards of material that kept Abigail from seeing the tears that had quickly formed at her words. She blinked quickly and turned to hang up the garment she was making for the woman. *Please, Lord, help me to hide how this woman's words have hurt. Please help me deal with all of this later.*

After Abigail's hatefulness to her, the fact that she didn't want to give her mother time to decide anything but was willing to stay a little longer for her own interests didn't surprise Meagan one bit. Nor did it seem to surprise her mother, for she said nothing as Abigail picked up *Godey's* magazine and flipped the pages.

"Here," she said, finding the fashion plate she liked. "I like this one."

It was a beautiful gown of gold and white brocade. "That will look lovely on you," Meagan said. "I believe I have fabric similar if not exactly like this."

She led the way to her stock of fabric on the shelves and pulled out several bolts. "Will this work for you?"

"Yes, I believe so. It looks like the fabric in the picture."

"I think it will work up beautifully."

"Very well, then. You have my measurements. When do you want me to come for the first fitting?"

Meagan looked at her appointment schedule once more. "I should be ready for your first fitting by next Friday afternoon about three."

Abigail nodded and pulled on her gloves. "Are you ready, Mother?"

"No, dear. If you can place an order with Miss Snow, I can, too. Sit down and have a cup of that delicious tea Mrs. Snow prepared. I have found a few gowns I want to talk to Miss Snow about."

Abigail shrugged and took a seat and the cup of tea Meagan's mother brought to her. She seemed quite content to be late, now that she'd said what she wanted to say. One glance at her told Meagan that she was feeling quite smug about the dart she'd shot into Meagan's heart.

Meagan was determined not to let her know how direct a hit she'd made. She managed to avoid looking at her, giving all of her attention to Mrs. Connors, instead. She couldn't help but wonder how Abigail had turned out the way she was when her mother was so gracious and kind.

The fashion plates Mrs. Connors chose were lovely, the afternoon dress in a brown print crepe and the dinner dress in a blue silk. It didn't take long for the woman to choose fabrics similar to the ones used in the pictures, and since she'd made an appointment for the next week, they decided she could come in for measurements then.

Meagan had never been so glad to pull down her CLOSED sign. She turned to her mother. "That is it for today. Abigail can ruin a day faster than anyone I know."

"I can understand that. Abigail Connors certainly is an unpleasant young woman," her mother said while gathering up the teacups. "I don't understand it at all. Her mother is very nice."

"She is. I think she was a bit. . ."

"Put out with her daughter. If Abigail had been younger, I think she'd have received a nice spanking. She could use one now, as far as I'm concerned. Your papa would never have let you girls talk to me the way she did her mama. Wonder what kind of man her father is?"

"He seemed very nice when I met him at the gala." Meagan shrugged. "Maybe her upbringing doesn't have anything to do with it. She just isn't a very pleasant person."

"Maybe there's a reason for it."

"I'm sure there is, Mama. There must be. Still, I wish I didn't have to have any dealings with her. Apparently, that isn't going to be the case."

That wasn't what was really bothering her, though. It was trying to come to grips with the fact that Abigail Connors was determined to marry Nate and had done all in her power to let Meagan know it.

&

Once a month or so, Nate had Natalie's grandparents and Abigail over for dinner. Rose had asked them over at least once a month for dinner when she was alive, and Nate had kept the practice up for Natalie's sake. He wished he could stop it—or at least stop asking Abigail—but he hadn't found a way to do it. He always hoped she'd have another engagement, but she never did.

When Abigail arrived early, informing him that her parents were under the weather and wouldn't be able to come, he felt a little put out that no one had notified him before now. He would have canceled until they felt better. He tried not to show his irritation that he evidently was going to have to spend the evening with Abigail. "I hope they are better soon. If I'd known, we could have put this off until next week."

"Oh, don't worry about it, Nate. I'm sure they will feel better very soon. They hated for Natalie to be disappointed, so I told them I would come."

Nate inhaled deeply, telling himself that he'd have to suffer through the evening on his own. He wasn't comfortable around Abigail when her family or friends weren't around. He had no doubt that she still wasn't happy with him for taking Meagan to the gala instead of her, yet she'd been overly sweet to him lately, and he was not sure what was going on with her.

Tonight she seemed her usual self during dinner, talking about the upcoming parties her friends had invited them to and a surprise birthday party she and her mother were planning for her father.

Natalie loved hearing all about the parties and Abigail's social life, listening intently to every word her aunt said. Nate had come to the conclusion that he'd rather Natalie *not* take after her aunt Abigail in that regard, however.

"Are you going to the party Jillian is hosting, Nate? If so, will you accompany me?" Abigail asked.

He shook his head. "I'm not planning on going to that, Abigail. I'm about partied out." And he had no desire at all to take her.

"But, Nate, you have to keep up with what is going on in town for the sake of the bank. Please reconsider," she implored him.

She'd used that reasoning on him too many times, and he was getting quite tired of it. "I do what I need to do for the sake of the bank, Abigail. I always have. I don't believe, however, that I have to attend every social event that comes along. I have a daughter to raise and—"

"Yes, and I'd like to talk to you about that," Abigail said, a slight smile on her lips.

Nate groaned to himself. He'd just given her an opening to talk about her favorite subject. . .and the one he most disliked. Well, he wasn't going to have that conversation in front of his daughter.

"Not right now, Abigail," he said as Mrs. Baker came in and served dessert.

"I understand. We'll talk later."

Nate had no doubt that they would. He'd given her the opening, and she wouldn't leave until she had her say. He might as well prepare himself for it.

They took turns playing checkers with Natalie after dinner, but finally, Nate could put it off no longer. "It's time to get ready for bed, Natalie, dear. I'll be up soon to hear your prayers."

"May I stay up a little longer, Papa? I'm having so much fun!"

If he hadn't wanted to get the inevitable conversation with Abigail over with, he might let her talk him into staying up later.

"Not tonight, dear," Abigail said before he had a chance to answer his daughter. "Your papa and I need to have a talk."

It was on the tip of his tongue to say that talk could wait a little longer and that Natalie could stay up, but he wanted the talk over with as much as Abigail wanted to start it. Probably even more so.

"Aunt Abigail is right, sweetie. You go on, and I'll be up soon."

"All right, Papa. Good night, Aunt Abby." She gave her aunt a hug.

"Good night, dear. Sweet dreams."

Nate watched his daughter scamper up the stairs before turning back to Abigail. She looked like a cat who'd swallowed a canary, thinking she was getting her way.

She sat down to pour the coffee his housekeeper had brought into the room and handed him a cup, as if she were the lady of the manor. She'd made him well aware that was what she wanted. But it was her dream—not his.

He sat down on a chair across from her. "What is it you wanted to talk about, Abigail?"

"Well, you brought it up, Nate, dear. You do have a child to raise, and you need help doing it. Natalie needs a mother."

He couldn't deny that—but he had someone he could see in that position, and it wasn't his sister-in-law. "Abigail, we've had this conversation many times."

"Yes, I know. Still, you don't seem to understand how badly a girl needs a mother. Nate, dear, just because you've taken over her wardrobe doesn't mean she doesn't need a mother. There are things you just aren't prepared to teach her and—" Abigail pulled a hankie from her sleeve and dabbed at her eyes. "Ever since the day Rose put Natalie in my arms and asked me to take care of her, I've felt as if she were mine."

The guilt and sorrow Nate felt that he hadn't been there to save his wife washed over him in waves, as it never failed to do when Abigail brought up that day. And when she did, he always felt even worse because his father-in-law thought he'd gone in and tried to save Rose, instead of just not being there in time. Abigail had let him think that, and when Nate wanted to tell him the truth, she'd talked him out of it, telling him that her father had gone through enough heartache in losing Rose, and they couldn't give him more.

"I think it's time we told your father the truth about the day Rose died. I was too late. I just didn't get there in time, and the house was in flames when I arrived. I don't know why you ever let him think I did. And I certainly don't know why I didn't correct it immediately! We need to tell him, Abigail."

"Nate, we can't do that! It would break his heart all over again. And what if he got so mad that he hadn't been told the truth that he fired you?"

"I'd be free from the guilt of not telling him the truth."

Abigail jumped to her feet and began to pace in front of his fireplace. "Well, we can't tell him now. Think of how it would hurt the family relationship! Besides, it would hurt my own relationship with him, Nate! I was only trying to protect you, to keep Father from blaming you for not being there—you know how hard he can be."

Actually, Jacob Connors had never shown that side to Nate, but Abigail seemed so distraught, Nate agreed not to tell her father the truth of that day. . .at least not yet.

"How did we get on this subject anyway?" Abigail asked. "We were discussing Natalie's need for a mother. How did we get to this?"

Nate sighed and shook his head. She'd brought up that day his life had changed forever. "Well, we aren't discussing it anymore," Nate said firmly.

"Nate. She needs a mother. She needs someone who is with her and will listen to her and give her advice and love her."

"Natalie has you and your mother, Abigail. It's not as if she has no women in her life. And that is the end of the discussion as far as I am concerned." He didn't mention that the Snow women had been a very good influence on his daughter, too. He had a feeling Abigail wouldn't take very well to that information just now. "I need to go up and hear Natalie's prayers. I'll see you home as soon as I do."

"No, Papa told the driver to come back for me at ten. It's nearly that now."

"That was thoughtful of Jacob. If I'm not down before the driver gets here, please tell your parents I hope they recover quickly."

"Yes. I will," she replied, her tone cool.

Nate knew she was angry with him again. She didn't even want to come up and kiss Natalie good night. Well, there was nothing to do about it except wait out her bad mood. She'd get past it eventually, and they'd have the same conversation again. That is the way it always was with Abigail.

thirteen

A few days later when Nate took Natalie for a fitting, she mentioned that her aunt Abigail had been grouchy lately. Nate hoped the woman hadn't taken her aggravation with him out on his daughter. "What has she seemed upset about?"

Natalie twisted her hands together and looked up at him. "She's sharp with me sometimes, and she doesn't want me to talk about Miss Meg anymore. She says that's all I talk about." Natalie did a good imitation of her aunt as she continued, "She said all she hears is 'Miss Meg this and Miss Meg that.' She said no one is that nice. But Papa, Miss Meg *is* that nice."

"Yes, she is. Your aunt Abigail just doesn't know her as well as we do, dear. Don't worry so about it."

"But Papa, I really like Miss Meg, and it's hard for me not to mention her name." Her eyes were big, brown, and sad.

"I'll talk to your aunt Abigail, Natalie. And I'm your papa. You can talk about Miss Meg all you want, anytime you want. I'll see that your aunt Abigail understands that." He flicked the reins to his horses and they took off in a brisk trot.

Natalie rewarded him with a huge smile. "Thank you, Papa!"

How dare Abigail tell Natalie that she didn't want her talking about Meagan! If Natalie had been misbehaving, that Abigail would admonish her would be one thing, but just because she was in a bad mood or didn't want to hear what the child had to say, why that was something entirely different!

By the time they arrived at Meagan's shop, Nate was very angry, but he tried not to let it show as she opened the door of the shop to them. "Good afternoon! I saw you coming around the porch."

She smiled at Natalie and at him, but her smile didn't seem as large or bright for him. Maybe it was just his imagination, or maybe his anger at Abigail was coloring his mood. He decided not to carry it into her shop. "Natalie has been looking forward to her fitting for days."

He didn't add that he had been looking forward to it, too. He just was not seeing enough of Meagan. He wanted to court her very much—but he was getting mixed messages from her and didn't know how to broach the subject. Still, he enjoyed watching her with his daughter.

He could hear giggling from behind the screen as Meagan helped her out of her day dress and into the new walking dress she was making for her. "Oh, it's beautiful, Miss Meg! I can't wait to wear it!"

"It is going to look lovely on you, Natalie."

"May I show Papa? I know the sleeves aren't in yet, but I'd like him to see it."

He heard Meagan chuckle at her enthusiasm. "Of course you may."

Natalie ran out from behind the screen and twirled in front of him. "Do you like it, Papa?"

It was a very pretty dress, and she looked adorable in it. He couldn't remember what kind of fabric Meagan had said it was, but it was of a red- and white-striped material that reminded him of a candy cane. "I do like it, Natalie! It looks wonderful on you."

"Thank you, kind sir." She giggled and curtsied, causing both him and Meagan to chuckle.

"Why, Natalie, dear, how nice that dress looks on you." Mrs. Snow entered the room with a smile. "Are you going to stay for dinner with us tonight?"

Natalie swung around to him. "Papa?"

Nate hesitated in answering, knowing his daughter wanted to stay, but waiting for Meagan to add her voice to the invitation as she normally did. Only she didn't, and the silence felt uncomfortable. "I think not tonight. But thank you for your invitation. Perhaps next time?"

"Of course. You and Natalie are always welcome at our table, Nate."

Nate waited a moment to see if Meagan would add anything to that. When she didn't, he simply said, "Thank you, Mrs. Snow. That means a lot to both Natalie and me."

"You are quite welcome. It's the least we can do after all you've done for us. Besides, we enjoy your company."

Somehow, Nate didn't think Meagan quite agreed with her mother, and he began to wonder if she'd gone to the gala with him because he gave them the loan. He sincerely hoped not.

❧

Frustrated that he didn't know how to approach Meagan and still upset at Abigail for telling Natalie not to talk about her, Nate went to see Abigail after work the next day.

Her housekeeper showed him into her parlor, and Abigail glided over to greet him. "Why, Nate, what a nice surprise. . . unless—is something wrong?"

Nate wondered if she could tell how upset he was by his expression. "There is something I would like to talk to you about."

"Oh?" She motioned to the settee. "Please, take a seat and

tell me what is on your mind."

Her voice sounded hopeful, and he hated to ruin her pleasant mood. He really did appreciate Abigail. She'd been there to help him with Natalie through her own grief. But she wanted him to feel something he didn't feel for her, and he wished she would just accept it. It would make being part of the same family so much easier. But as he knew all too well, life wasn't always easy, and it was for his daughter's sake he was here today. He might as well get straight to it. He took the chair beside the settee and waited for Abigail to sit down before he said anything.

"Natalie says you don't want her talking about Miss Snow anymore."

"What?" Her right eyebrow went up as it always did when she felt defensive.

"Did you not tell her that you didn't want her talking about Miss Snow?" He knew that Natalie didn't lie. He waited for Abigail's answer, well aware that he couldn't rule out that she would.

"Perhaps she misunderstood me, Nate. I did tell her that Miss Meg seemed to be all she wanted to talk about anymore."

"She likes Miss Snow and considers her a friend. It's no different than you talking about your friends all the time."

"It is different, Nate."

"How so?" Let her explain further if she would.

"It just is. She seems quite taken with the woman, Nate. I don't want her to get hurt. You might want to guard against Natalie becoming too attached to her—she's a mere seamstress!"

If he only knew how Meagan felt about him, Nate would gladly tell Abigail that if he had his way, Natalie would be seeing much more of the *seamstress*. But something in his sister-in-law's demeanor kept him from doing so. He did make one thing clear. "I don't want you ever to tell Natalie that she can't talk about someone she cares about. If she can't feel free to talk to you, then how can you possibly think you are—"

"Oh, Nate dear," Abigail interrupted him, her tone suddenly sweet as honey. "This has just been a misunderstanding on Natalie's part. I will tell her I never meant to upset her and assure her that she can always talk to me about anything."

Nate stood. He felt he'd accomplished the main thing he came here for. He was pretty certain that Abigail wouldn't be telling Natalie that she couldn't talk about Meagan or anyone else she might wish to talk about again.

❧

If Meagan's mother had wondered why she hadn't insisted that Nate and Natalie stay for supper, she hadn't said anything, and for that Meagan was very grateful. She didn't know why she hadn't tried to get them to stay. . . . Well, maybe she did. She just wasn't sure how Nate felt about her. There was a time when she'd thought he might care about her as much as she did him, but Abigail's insinuations had her doubting his motivation in asking her to the gala. Had it only been to help her business out that he'd asked her to accompany him?

Meagan hoped not. She prayed not. But there was no denying that it well could have been for that reason. He hadn't asked her to accompany him anywhere else, so how could she be sure? And if he was not interested in her in the way she was him, it was better for her to steel her heart against the love she could no longer deny she felt for him.

Meagan kept telling herself that as she cut out the muslin pattern for Abigail's new gown. Oh, how she wished she could tell the woman to take her business elsewhere. But for the sake of her business and her family's future, she could not. It was time to face reality and quit dreaming.

She was face-to-face with reality when Abigail came in for her fitting that very afternoon. She'd brought a friend with her, Miss Rebecca Dodson.

"Oh, what a nice little shop you have here," Miss Dodson said. "I've been hearing all kinds of good things about your work. I'm still using Mrs. Sparrow for now, but Abigail insisted I come with her and keep her company."

Meagan was immensely relieved that the woman had a dressmaker of her own. She liked Mrs. Connors a lot, but her daughter was another matter entirely, and Meagan wasn't interested in acquiring any of Abigail's friends as customers.

"Please, make yourself comfortable, then. There are some of the latest fashion magazines to look at, or if you and Miss Connors prefer to talk, she'll be able to hear you through the screen."

Evidently, that is what they did prefer because she'd barely started pinning the muslin on Abigail before she began to talk about Nate.

"Nate came by to see me yesterday afternoon, right out of the blue, Rebecca," Abigail said.

"Oh? What did he want?"

"He is concerned about Natalie. He wants her to be able to come to both of us with anything. He said he wants her to be able to talk about the things that mean a lot to her."

"Hmm. That sounds as if he's. . .thinking about the future, doesn't it?" Miss Dodson asked.

"I certainly hope so!" Abigail giggled, and Meagan had to struggle to keep from purposely sticking her with the pin she was holding.

"I've been telling him how much Natalie needs a mother. Perhaps he's finally taking me seriously," Abigail continued.

Her friend laughed. "And I know just who you have in mind."

"Well, who better to raise Natalie than the sister of her mother?"

"You have a point. Besides, Natalie has always been close to you, and you've loved Nate for a very long time."

Meagan took the pins out of her mouth and swallowed hard. She was glad she was behind Abigail so that the woman couldn't see the tears that formed. Abigail was trying to get a message across to her; there was no doubt about it. Well, it appeared she did have a prior claim to Nate, and no amount of wishing or dreaming was going to change that. It was time Meagan accepted the fact that she would never have a future with Nate Brooks. She blinked back the tears, stuck the pins back in her mouth, and finished pinning the pattern on Abigail. By the time she was done, Meagan had her tears under control and was resolved to get through the afternoon. Knowing she wouldn't be able to do it on her own, she prayed silently for help to do just that.

"I think that's it. The gown is going to fit you nicely, Miss Connors. Now all I have to do is mark the pins and take them out. You can come back for a fitting a week from today, if that is convenient for you."

"That will be fine," Abigail said. "I think Nate will really like it."

The woman loved to shoot darts, and her aim was perfect, Meagan thought. Oh, how she wished she never had to pin another thing on her! But she couldn't get out of it. There was still the loan to pay off and the fact that Abigail could cause problems with that loan—not to mention her customers.

Over half of them were Nate and Abigail's friends or business acquaintances. No. Much as she would like to tell the woman to find someone else to sew for her, she just couldn't do it. All she could do was pray for the strength to keep her thoughts to herself. . .and to put Nate Brooks out of her mind.

fourteen

Nate was on the way to Meagan's shop with Natalie for a fitting when he realized that he wasn't going to have an excuse to go to her shop much longer. At least, not nearly as often. There wasn't much more he could have Meagan make Natalie. She had nearly a whole new wardrobe.

He'd hoped it would become obvious to Meagan that part of the reason he'd ordered so much from her was so that he could see her on a semiregular basis. . .especially after he'd taken her to the Crescent. He thought she would be aware that he wanted to court her. If she'd come to that conclusion, she certainly showed no sign of it. Feeling that his time was running out, he was determined to find a way to tell her how he felt and that he wanted to see more of her.

He hoped to have that chance today. His daughter had come to feel so comfortable and welcome at Meagan's shop and home that she ran ahead of him and burst into the shop. He could hear their conversation as he approached the door.

"Good afternoon, Miss Meg! I'm here for my fitting!" he heard Natalie say.

He heard Meagan chuckle. "So you are," she said. "Good afternoon to you! I have everything ready, so come on and we'll get started."

Nate entered the shop just as they disappeared behind the changing screen. He took his normal seat in one of the chairs and waited for Natalie to come around the screen and twirl in front of him. When she did, it was worth the wait. She looked adorable in the silk dress she could wear for dinner or to church. Meagan only needed to put the hem in and finish the matching jacket.

Natalie twirled this way and that in front of the mirror, admiring herself.

"I think she likes it," Meagan said.

He chuckled. "Now whatever gave you that idea? She looks adorable, Meagan. And she loves everything you've made her."

"Thank you. She's a pleasure to sew for."

Mrs. Snow entered the room just then. "Oh, Natalie dear, I knew that would look lovely on you, and it does!"

Natalie curtsied prettily. "Thank you, Mrs. Snow. I feel like a princess in everything Miss Meg makes for me."

"And you look like one," Nate added.

"Nate, it's good to see you. Are you able to stay for supper with us?"

"Oh, Papa, can we? Please?"

His daughter's eyes implored him to say yes, but he wasn't sure what to do—

"Please do join us," Meagan said, looking at Natalie.

Nate wondered why she didn't look at him and had a feeling she'd added her invitation to her mother's just for Natalie's sake, but he wasn't going to turn it down. Hopefully it would give him the opportunity to be able to talk to her later. "Thank you, then. We'd be honored to join you."

❧

As she and her sisters helped get the meal of roast pork, mashed potatoes, and green beans on the table, Meagan wondered why she hadn't told her mother earlier in the day not to ask Nate and Natalie to stay for supper. Once the invitation was issued, however, she couldn't bear disappointing Natalie again. She kept telling herself that it was the child she was concerned with, yet if she were being honest with herself, she had to admit that she truly wanted them to stay—in spite of the fact that Abigail was making her life miserable each and every time she came into the shop.

Meagan had come to the realization that Nate hadn't meant to hurt her. It wasn't his fault that she'd begun to care for him so much. She shouldn't have read so much into the outing for a soda or the invitation to the Crescent gala. . .or the dance lessons in the moonlight. She told herself that the first had just been out of politeness and the second had most likely been to help her business out. The third, well, he hadn't given her any real encouragement that he cared about her the way she did him. Not really. She'd just hoped.

And now, looking at Nate from across her dining room table as they all enjoyed the apple pie her mother had made earlier in the day, she told herself to let go of the hope. Much as she cared for Nate and his daughter, his sister-in-law was part of their family and there was really no way to compete with Abigail Connors. She was a determined woman, and she wanted Nate. Of that there was no doubt. She'd come out and told Meagan that she planned to be married to him. How much plainer could it be? If Abigail was that certain, she must know how Nate felt about her.

Yet the way Nate looked at Meagan, off and on throughout the meal, continued to make her pulse race and turn her heart to mush. When he asked if he could have a minute with her after supper, while Sarah, Becca, and Natalie were helping to clear the table, she wasn't sure what to think. All a tremble on the inside, she led him to the family parlor where they'd had tea the day he'd decided to give them the loan.

She motioned for him to take a seat in the same chair he'd sat in the first time he'd come to this room, and she seated herself on the settee. "What is it you want to talk to me about, Nate?"

"It's of a personal nature, Meagan."

"Oh?" Her heart seemed to stop the slow somersault it had begun, and she held her breath, waiting for his reply.

"For some time now, I've wanted to ask you to have dinner with me. There is a new restaurant in town that I've wanted to try, and I'd very much like to take you with me if you would like to go. I was wondering if you would be free to accompany me tomorrow evening."

Oh how she wanted to go! With every fiber of her being, she wanted to accept his invitation. But from all of Abigail's accounts, they were practically engaged. If so, he certainly shouldn't be asking her to go to dinner with him. Who did he think he was? He might be the banker who loaned her money to start her business, but he was also the man who'd stolen her heart when he was almost engaged to another. Nate had no business playing with her feelings.

She might be risking her business, but she couldn't risk more heartache. Disappointment in him pierced her heart as she jumped up from the settee and answered, "I'm sorry, but I won't be able to accompany you, Nate." Meagan was well aware that she sounded angry, but she couldn't help it. She was.

Nate stood also, looking a bit surprised and. . .there was something else in his eyes as he looked at her. "I'm sorry. I—"

The girls entered just then, and Meagan didn't know who was the more relieved at the interruption—she or Nate.

"Papa, may I play one game of checkers with Becca? I'm getting much better at it, and I know it is from playing with her," Natalie said.

Nate glanced at Meagan and then back to his daughter.

He shook his head. "Not tonight, dear. We need to be getting home."

Meagan's heart twisted in her chest. She didn't want things to end like this between her and Nate. She didn't want them to go. But they weren't hers to keep, and it was becoming more painful by the day to want something so badly and know that she couldn't have it. A life with Nate and Natalie wasn't going to happen for her, and she had to accept that fact. Abigail had a stronger claim, and there was nothing Meagan could do about it except perhaps to lower her standards—and that was something she had no intention of doing.

❧

Nate listened to Natalie's prayers, trying to hide his heartache at Meagan's refusal to have dinner with him. But his daughter was quite intuitive and put her small hands on each side of his face as he kissed her good night. "Papa, are you all right? You seem sad tonight."

He was sad. But he didn't want his daughter taking on his mood and becoming dispirited herself. "I'm fine, dear. Just a little tired, I suppose."

Nate told himself that it wasn't really a lie. He was tired of being lonely and tired of not knowing what direction the Lord wanted him to go in. He'd thought it was to pursue Meagan Snow, but after tonight, he thought that perhaps he'd been wrong.

"Well, you'd better turn in yourself and get a good night's rest," Natalie advised with a giggle.

"I might just do that, sweetheart. You sleep tight and have sweet dreams."

"You, too, Papa," Natalie said as he turned down the gas-light and left her door ajar so he could hear if she called out in the night.

He went back downstairs and entered his study to find that his housekeeper had left him a pot of hot cocoa. Mrs. Baker knew he liked the beverage any time of year and especially before bed. Perhaps it would help him sleep, but he doubted he'd have sweet dreams tonight. It appeared that he'd been living on dreams ever since he met Meagan Snow. At first, she'd reminded him of his Rose, and then as he'd come to know her, she'd become a gracious, beautiful woman in her own right—at least in his thoughts and dreams. But when she'd turned down his invitation to dinner, he'd come to the realization that perhaps she wasn't interested in him as a man, but only as the one who had approved her bank loan.

No, he told himself. That was being unfair to her. She'd never acted as if she was only kind to him because he was a banker. He knew she cared about Natalie, and he'd come to think she might care about him. But perhaps that was only wishful thinking on his part. Perhaps she simply was not impressed with the man he was.

She was used to being around real people instead of the kind he'd introduced her to at the gala. Most of them were superficial, going about their days with only one thing in mind: to be entertained, to have a good time. Why, most of the people he'd associated with since Rose's death had too much time on their hands, and they didn't use it for much good.

He wanted something different for himself and his daughter. Perhaps he'd read too much into Meagan's refusal tonight. The girls had interrupted them before he could find out why she was turning him down. Meagan had looked weary. Maybe that was all it was. She worked very hard, and if the conversation at the supper table had been any indication, her business was growing. Perhaps she was just tired and had a lot of work to do.

Nate leaned back in his office chair and took a sip of cocoa. It was still very warm and comforting. He took another sip and began to feel better. He wasn't going to give up on Meagan—not now—and not until he had no other choice.

fifteen

Meagan barely managed to make small talk with her mother and sisters after Nate and Natalie left. She didn't want them to see how upset she was. She flipped through one of her newest magazines while she kept them company in the parlor. That way she didn't have to look up every time they asked her a question and she answered or made a comment.

"Mr. Brooks seemed in a hurry to leave tonight, didn't he, Meagan?" Becca looked up while she and Sarah played a game of checkers in the family parlor. "Natalie asked if we could play a game of checkers, but he barely let her finish her cookie before they took off."

"Maybe he had work to do at home, dear," her mother answered.

"He didn't look too happy about leaving," Sarah said. "Did you make him angry, Meagan?"

Her sister's question took her by surprise, and Meagan inhaled sharply. *Did I? Well, if so, it was no more so than he'd made me.* The more Meagan thought about their conversation the more upset she became, and she was glad her mother spoke, saving her from having to answer her sister.

"Meagan make Mr. Brooks angry?" Their mother chuckled. "Now, Sarah, you know better. Your sister goes out of her way not to anger anyone."

"I know. But he looked. . ." She shrugged. "I don't know. He just didn't look as happy when he left as when he came in for supper."

"Hmm," Mama said. "I'm sure he's fine, dear. He probably just wanted to get Natalie home and ready for bed. And that's just what you girls need to be doing now. Don't you have some studying to do?"

"I do have a test at the end of the week," Sarah admitted.

"Well, go on, then. I'll be up to say good night soon."

Meagan was relieved the conversation about Nate had ended. Just hearing his name made her want to cry. She released a sigh and turned to leave the parlor. "I think I'll go straighten up the shop, Mama."

"Have a cup of tea with me first, dear," her mother said. "You haven't had much time to relax lately."

"That sounds good." Meagan followed her mother into the kitchen.

Once they sat down at the table with their tea, her mother said, "Tell me what's bothering you, dear. You've looked so sad this evening."

"Oh, Mama." Meagan sighed and shook her head. "It will do no good to discuss it."

"It's as I suspect, then. It's matters of the heart you are dealing with."

She should have known she couldn't keep anything from her mother. At her gentle words, Meagan began to talk about it all. "Nate asked me to go to dinner with him tomorrow evening, and I turned him down."

"But why, dear? I know you care for the man."

"And so does Abigail Connors. She is determined to have him, Mama. And from what she tells me, she's practically engaged to him. She's let me know in no uncertain terms that she plans to marry the man."

"But that could just be her dream, dear."

"Mama, she sees him all the time. If she didn't believe it,

then why would she say it?"

"Perhaps she said it to keep you from accepting a dinner invitation from him?"

Oh, how badly Meagan wanted to grasp at the hope her mother was handing her. But she was too afraid to. Yet there was a flicker. . . . "Mama, do you think that could be true?"

"I think it could be, yes. But I could be wrong. You are right to protect your heart, dear. But while doing that, you need to realize that not all things are as they seem."

"I've been hoping that she was just trying to upset me. But Mama, she is his sister-in-law and Natalie's aunt. She will always be part of his family, a tie that I do not have."

"I understand that. Still, true love is very strong. I do not get the impression that Mr. Brooks is smitten with Abigail Connors. And I can't think that he would ask you to dinner if that were so. But I don't have all the answers except the most important one."

"What is that, Mama?"

"You know yourself what it is, my Meggie. Take it all to the Lord, and trust in Him to work it out."

Meagan nodded. "I will, Mama. I'm going to straighten up the shop and then turn in. Thank you for listening to me."

"I'm always here for you, dear."

Meagan kissed the top of her mother's head. "I know you are. And I don't know what any of us would do without you."

She started to rinse her cup and saucer, but her mother shooed her out of the kitchen. "I'll do this. You go take care of the shop, and spend a little time with the Lord."

Meagan did just that, praying as she worked. She didn't know what the Lord's plan for her and Nate was. Hearing Abigail go on about her and Nate and the places they'd gone and the future she hoped for—it was hard not to believe her. Yet. . .there was a look in Nate's eyes tonight that had made Meagan want to cry. He seemed disappointed that she refused his invitation. Perhaps he was. But even if he was, that didn't mean he wasn't planning a future with Abigail. Meagan simply did not know what was going on, and she prayed that the Lord would help her through the pain if there was no future for them.

❧

Nate and Natalie had supper at the Connors' home several nights later, and to his happy surprise, Abigail wasn't there. It was a rare event when she wasn't at her parents' house when Nate and Natalie came for dinner.

"Where is Aunt Abby tonight, Grandmother?" Natalie asked when they entered the dining room.

"A friend of hers is having a dinner just for the women they socialize with. Caroline Atwell has become engaged to be married, and it's a celebration of sorts," Georgette informed her once they were at the dinner table.

"I'm sure they'll have a delightful time," Nate said. He had noticed that the women Abigail was with most of the time just loved to talk about weddings.

"I'm sure Aunt Abby will enjoy helping to plan the wedding," Natalie said.

Nate was sure of it, too. The only thing she'd like better would be to be planning her own wedding to him. The cook served them Natalie's favorite meal of chicken and dumplings, with peas and baby onions on the side. Fluffy rolls completed the course.

As the meal progressed, Nate began to relax and enjoy himself. He could only wish Abigail had more outings with her friends on the nights that he and Natalie were invited to her parents' home for dinner. Then he felt bad at that thought. Abigail had been a great blessing to him right after Rose passed away. It was only in the last few years that he'd realized she wanted to replace her sister in his affections. That was something he was finding very hard to think about at all. Especially as he'd already put Meagan Snow in that position. . .even if she didn't return his feelings.

Natalie's laugh brought him out of his depressing thoughts. She did enjoy being around her grandparents.

"Oh, Grandpa, that was funny," Natalie said. "Will you play checkers with me after dinner? I'm getting much better at them."

"Of course I will. Soon we'll have to teach you to play chess," Jacob said.

"I'd love to learn chess!" Natalie said. "But I want to beat you and Papa at checkers before I do."

The cook came in to clear the table and serve bread pudding and coffee.

"Oh, thank you," Natalie said as her dessert was placed in front of her. "Everything has been delicious! Thank you for making my favorites!"

"You're welcome," the Connorses' cook said. "Your grandmother asked me to make them especially for you, Miss Natalie."

"Thank you, Grandmother. It's probably a good thing Aunt Abby wasn't here tonight. You know how she feels about dumplings!"

"You are welcome, dear. And yes, I do know how your aunt Abigail feels about them. She doesn't like them very much, does she?"

Natalie giggled. "No, she sure doesn't."

"But you know what?"

Natalie shook her head. "What, Grandmother?"

"She would have had to fill up on peas and onions, because I was going to serve it anyway. The best thing about her being otherwise engaged this evening is that we haven't had to hear her complain about the meal."

Everyone got a chuckle out of that, even the cook who was placing Nate's dessert in front of him. Georgette was exactly right. Abigail would have complained all evening. That his in-laws loved Natalie very much was always apparent, and tonight was no exception.

"You may call it a night, Mrs. Jackson. Natalie will help with the cleanup."

"Thank you, ma'am. Everything is washed and put up except what's on the table."

"Thank you." Georgette smiled at the woman. "Have a nice evening."

"I will. Good night."

Nate and Jacob retired to the study while Natalie and her grandmother cleared the table after dessert. "It's always a pleasure to have you and Natalie over, Nate. It brings a little life into this house."

"It's been a most enjoyable evening, Jacob. Natalie loves coming over." He did, too, most of the time. It was only Abigail's company that put him on edge at times. But he was thankful for Jacob and Georgette. "I'm blessed that you and Georgette have always been so kind to me and welcomed me as much as you do Natalie."

"Nate, you are like a son to us. You are the father of our only granddaughter. You'll always be part of this family. But you need a life outside of us, too. You need to remarry, son. You need to for your sake *and* Natalie's."

He could honestly answer Jacob. "I've been thinking about it." The only problem was, Nate couldn't help but feel that

Jacob was hinting for him to marry Abigail. He couldn't blame the man. He wanted his daughter to be happy, too. And he wanted to keep his granddaughter close to the family. Nate understood all of that. He just wasn't sure he could give Jacob and Abigail what they wanted. He wasn't sure at all. The only woman he wanted as a wife was Meagan Snow, and if he couldn't get her to go to dinner with him, he didn't know how it was going to be possible to ask her to become his wife. He could think about getting married all he wanted, but at the moment, it didn't look like marriage would ever be to the woman he'd come to love.

❧

Later, after they'd returned home and Natalie was ready for bed, Nate went up to tuck her in. They both knelt beside her bed as she said her prayers.

"Dear Father, thank You for this day and for everyone I love. Especially Papa. Thank You for my grandparents and for Aunt Abby, too. Please forgive me for the things I did wrong today and help me to do better tomorrow. Thank You for everything—especially for Jesus. Amen."

Nate was always touched by her simple prayers, and he had a feeling that the Lord was, too. Natalie scrambled up into her bed and pulled the covers up around her neck.

"Did you have a good time at your grandparents' tonight?" Nate asked as he brushed his lips across her brow.

"I did. I love playing checkers with Grandfather. I'm glad he doesn't let me win. I want to beat him fair and square one day!"

"I'm sure you will. You are getting better all the time." Nate sat down on the side of the bed and thought a minute before he spoke. "Natalie, dear, would you like for me to marry again one of these days?"

She sat straight up in bed and clapped her hands. "Oh, Papa, yes I would! I would love to have a mama like all of my friends! It would be so nice!"

"Do you think so?"

"Oh, yes! And you wouldn't be so lonesome when I grow up or when I'm not here."

Now how did she know I get lonesome? Nate wondered. "Well, I'll tell you what. I will do some thinking about it, all right?"

"Oh, yes, Papa. Please do think about it!"

She settled back down on her pillow, and Nate kissed her once more before turning down the light and going back down to his study.

He had been thinking about marriage a lot lately. Abigail had been bringing up the subject more often over the last few months, but it was Meagan he envisioned as his bride. But if Meagan didn't care about him the same way, what was he to do?

Abigail had been right about Natalie. She did need and want a mother. Yet the only woman he wanted to fill that position seemed cool and distant to him. Until the other day, he truly thought Meagan was beginning to care about him, too. Now he wasn't so sure.

He didn't want to give up on Meagan yet. Maybe she was just having a bad day when he asked her to dinner. That might be all it was. Natalie had her last fitting set for the next day. Perhaps he would be able to ask Meagan out again. If she turned him down this time, well then, he'd just have to accept that he'd been mistaken about how she might feel toward him and get over her.

But he wasn't ready to give up tonight. He bowed his head and asked for guidance. "Dear Lord, I'm in a quandary here. I have no idea if Meagan cares for me as I do her, but I need to find out. My daughter wants a mother, and I need a wife. I want it to be Meagan. But if that is not Your will, please help me to accept what is and go on. In Jesus' precious name, I pray. Amen."

sixteen

Meagan greeted Natalie and Nate when they came in the shop on Saturday morning, feeling both sad and relieved that this was Natalie's last fitting for a while. Much as she loved this child—and her papa—it had become painful to see them both when she knew they would never be hers.

"Good afternoon, Natalie. Are you ready to try on your new dress?"

"Oh, yes, I am!" Natalie hurried behind the changing screen. "I can't wait to wear it to church."

Meagan's mother came in with a pot of coffee and tray of cookies just then. She'd known the Brookses were coming, and Meagan had asked her to bring in some cookies for the child.

"Good morning, Nate. Would you like some coffee while Natalie is trying on her outfit?"

"Good morning, Mrs. Snow. I'd love a cup. It is such a beautiful spring day out. I think I'll take Natalie over to Basin Park after lunch. They sprayed the streets this morning to keep down the dust, so even if a breeze comes up, it should be pleasant out. A concert band is performing today, and I've heard they are very good."

"It's been awhile since I've gone over there, but it is a nice day for it. I'm sure Natalie will enjoy it."

While her mother was entertaining Nate, Meagan helped Natalie change out of her walking dress and into her new lightweight wool church dress. Before she sent the child out to show her papa, Natalie motioned for her to bend down.

"Guess what, Miss Meg?" she whispered in her ear.

"I don't know. What is it?" Meagan whispered back.

Natalie cupped both hands around her mouth as she got close to Meagan's ear. "My papa is thinking about getting married again!"

Trying to hide the pain that splintered her chest at the child's excited whisper, Meagan asked, "Are you happy about that?"

Natalie smiled and nodded. "I'll have a mommy like all of my friends. And Papa won't be so sad all the time."

If Nate was thinking of remarrying, Meagan was certain it was to Abigail. After all, that was all she'd been hearing from the woman for weeks now. She didn't quite know for whom her heart was breaking—herself or Natalie. The child did need a mother, and it was obvious that she wanted one badly. But even if Meagan hadn't wanted Nate for herself, she'd be disappointed in his choice of a wife and mother. Abigail was not the woman Meagan could imagine Nate with, and she certainly couldn't picture the woman being the kind of mother Natalie needed.

But the decision wasn't hers to make, and it appeared that Nate had already made it. She prayed for the Lord to help her accept that her dreams weren't going to come true and to not let Nate see how brokenhearted she was.

She gave the child a hug and sent her out to show her finished dress to her papa.

"Natalie, you look too grown-up," Nate said. "I can see that I'm going to have to watch you closely around all those suitors who'll be coming to our door a few years down the road."

"Oh, Papa," Natalie said with a laugh. "You are silly. I don't like any old boys, and they don't like me. They are too busy catching frogs to notice what I'm wearing!"

Nate laughed. "Well, that's quite a relief. They'll be noticing much sooner than I'll be ready for them to."

"Oh, Papa!" Natalie giggled again. "Are Becca and Sarah here? May I go show them my new dress?"

"I believe they are upstairs, but you may go, if it is all right with your papa," Mrs. Snow said. "Be sure to get a cookie before you leave."

"I will. Thank you!" Natalie said as she ran into the foyer and up the stairs, calling, "Becca! Sarah!"

Meagan was thankful that her mother remained in the room, but her relief was short lived as the knocker on the front door sounded. Her mother went to answer the door, leaving Meagan and Nate together.

"I—I'm not sure Natalie and I are going to know what to do, now that her wardrobe is filled for this season. She's growing much too fast to have you make anything for fall."

Relieved that the conversation centered on Natalie, Meagan felt herself relax a bit. "Yes, she certainly is. I did put deep hems in everything I've made her so that it won't be a problem should they need to be let down."

"Thank you. I do appreciate that." Nate's glance caught hers. "Meagan, you'd mentioned once that you liked to close the shop early on Saturdays, if possible. Do you think— would you be able to go to lunch with Natalie and me and then to Basin Park to hear the concert today?"

For a moment, Meagan's heart sang with joy at his invitation—then it plummeted. How dare he ask her to spend the day with him and Natalie when he was practically betrothed to another woman? She steeled her heart for what she had to do, no matter how badly it pounded for her to accept his invitation.

"No, thank you." She knew her voice sounded very cool. The look of disappointment in his eyes was almost her undoing, but she had to remain strong if she was to avoid even more heartache. "I'll not be able to do that."

❧

Nate's heart felt as if a vise were squeezing it. It appeared that Meagan had no interest in going out with him. . .yet she looked so sad. He had to ask. "Meagan, have I done anything to offend you? If so, please tell me and please forgive me."

"I. . .you. . ." Meagan shook her head as Natalie rushed back into the room in her new dress with Becca following close behind. She gave her attention to the girls, and Nate tried to do the same. It appeared he wasn't going to get any answers—at least not today.

"Becca wants a dress like this one, Miss Meg," Natalie said as she went behind the screen.

"Oh does she now?" Meagan asked. "I'll see what I can do, Becca. Think about what color you would want."

Nate didn't hear the rest of the conversation as Natalie went behind the screen to change and Meagan went to help.

"Good day, Mr. Brooks," Becca said. "Natalie said you are going to Basin Park today. She's very excited about it."

"Yes, we are going after lunch. It's quite nice out even for early June, so we're going to take advantage of the sunny skies and balmy day."

"Papa?" Natalie said from behind the screen.

"Yes, dear?"

"Could Becca come with us?"

Why not? Nate thought. Her sister certainly didn't want to. He looked at Becca and could tell that she really wanted to go. "We'd love to have you come with us and share lunch with us. Sarah is welcome to come, too, if she'd like. Run ask your mother—or better yet, let's both go ask your mother if you can accompany us."

"Oh, thank you, Mr. Brooks. I've done my chores this morning, so perhaps she'll say yes!"

Nate heard Natalie from behind the screen. "Do you think you could come too, Miss Meg? It's going to be such fun!"

He held his breath, waiting to see what Meagan said. "I'm afraid not, Natalie. But it was nice of you to ask Becca. I know she will enjoy it."

He followed Becca out of the room. There was no need to hear any more. The disappointment Nate felt dug deep into his heart. For whatever reason, Meagan wanted nothing to do with him socially. He was going to have to accept it and get on with his life.

❧

Meagan didn't know how she managed to refuse Natalie's invitation. She *wanted* to spend the afternoon with Natalie and her father. *Wanted* to go to lunch with them and then over to Basin Park to hear the concert. Yet it would only mean more heartache for her.

She helped Natalie change back into the dress she'd worn to the shop and then carefully folded the outfit she'd made her and wrapped it in tissue and placed it in a bag. "I hope you'll enjoy your new dress as much as I enjoyed making it for you. If the hem needs to be taken down, I'll be glad to do that for you."

"I'll wear it to church tomorrow!" Natalie promised.

Meagan was relieved that her mother came back into the shop with Nate, Becca, and Sarah. That way she wouldn't have to speak to him alone. She had no idea what to say to him anymore.

"I have some shopping to do this afternoon," her mother

said. "I can meet you at the park and bring the girls home. That way you won't have to go out of your way to bring them back."

Thank you, Mama. Meagan wasn't sure she could face seeing Nate again that day. It hurt too much to see the look in his eyes.

"I don't mind bringing them home, Mrs. Snow."

"I know you don't, and I appreciate your willingness to get them back, but I'll meet you there about two, if that is all right."

"That will be fine. The concert should be about over by that time."

"I'll see you then. Thank you again for asking them. They don't get many outings like this."

"Natalie is thrilled to have some company other than her boring papa, I believe," he said. He stood a moment as if he didn't quite know what else to say.

Meagan's mother rounded up the girls and led them outside. *Dear Mama, she is trying to make this all easier on me.* Yet Meagan knew that nothing was going to help her heart stop aching—at least not yet, and probably not for months to come.

Meagan handed Nate the bag with Natalie's dress in it. "If the hem needs to be taken down, I'll be glad to do that for this or any of her other frocks."

"Thank you. I'll remember," Nate said, taking the bag from her.

Their fingers brushed, and the electric shock that flowed from the tips of her fingers straight to her heart astounded Meagan. She couldn't help but wonder if Nate had felt it, too. If so, he didn't mention it as he followed her mother and the excited girls out the door. But he turned back with a look in his eyes that almost had her changing her mind and saying she'd go with them. It was only with the Lord's help that she bit her tongue.

He did look disappointed—just like she felt. Only she was disappointed in him. That he could be involved with someone else and pursuing her at the same time. . .well, she just couldn't understand it. She'd thought he was much more honorable than that. Still, he looked so sad.

Could she be wrong about it all? With Abigail talking about how much time she spent with Nate and Natalie and that she expected to be married to him by next year. . .why would she be telling Meagan and anyone else within hearing distance about it if it weren't true? Could she just have wanted Meagan to think that so that she wouldn't accept Nate's invitations?

Surely not. No. That is just wishful thinking on my part, Meagan told herself. Yet. . .should she have done what she truly wanted to do and gone to lunch with him and Natalie? She stood at the side of the window and watched as Nate helped all of the girls into his buggy, her mother looking on.

No. She did what she had to do for her own sake, but her heart broke as she watched him drive away.

seventeen

During the next couple of weeks, Nate thought about the last few months repeatedly. He didn't see how he could have offended Meagan. He'd only wanted to see more of her. He hadn't treated her or her family badly. He liked them much too much to do so. The only thing he could come up with that made any sense at all to him was that Meagan Snow just was not interested in him the way he was in her. Yet when she'd refused his invitation to lunch that day, she'd looked. . .almost as sad as he felt. *Sad*. How could that be, and why?

All Nate really knew was that his dreams of a life with Meagan weren't coming true, and he had to get on with life. It didn't help him at all that Natalie kept asking when they were going to visit the Snows. He had no reason to take her now that Meagan had finished her wardrobe for the spring and well into the summer. He could only hope that Natalie grew enough to need the hems in her dresses let down an inch or so.

Life seemed to have reverted back to where it was before he'd met Meagan and her family, only Nate felt his loneliness as he'd never felt it before. He was even thankful for the invitation to Abigail's for dinner that evening.

One thing he'd found out about himself was that he didn't want to be alone for the rest of his life. He was extremely grateful that he had Natalie, but she would grow up, get married, and start a family of her own one day. Then he would be all by himself except for when invited to dinner or when they came to visit him.

Nate shook his head to rid himself of his maudlin thoughts. Natalie was still a little girl, and it would be a long time before all of that happened. But even now, he longed for someone to share his life with, and he knew Natalie wanted a mother. He'd loved Rose with all his heart, and then Meagan had come along. That he was in love with her there was no doubt. But she obviously didn't return those feelings. . .and he didn't think the love he'd felt for Rose and then for Meagan would come more than twice in a lifetime. Was it possible that he could learn to care about someone enough to share his life with her? Natalie did need a mother.

He sighed as he stopped his rig outside Abigail's and hitched his horse to the post. He helped Natalie down and watched as she ran to her aunt's door. He was a bit surprised when Abigail opened the door herself. She enveloped Natalie in a hug and then smiled up at him.

"I'm so glad you could come. I haven't seen you in several days."

Her words seemed balm to his battered ego. At least Abigail was glad to see him. Normally he wouldn't have been thrilled that it was just the three of them for dinner, but tonight he was relieved that he didn't have to put up with her friends.

It was a surprisingly relaxed atmosphere. Instead of eating in the dining room, Abigail had set a smaller table in her parlor for just the three of them, and there was much more of a family feel to the evening than her elaborate parties. The first course was mulligatawny soup, followed by veal cutlets with brown sauce, rice, potatoes, and string beans.

"This is very good, Aunt Abby," Natalie said.

"Thank you, dear. Of course, when Millie knew you were coming, she took extra care. She wondered if you would like to help her make some cookies after supper."

"May I? Papa loves gingersnaps. Could we make those?"

"Of course you may. And you can take some home with you, too."

"Thank you, Aunt Abby!"

Any hopes Nate had of leaving early disappeared, but Natalie was happy and excited, and he supposed there were worse things than spending an evening in Abigail's company. Being alone and spending too much time thinking of Meagan, for instance. Perhaps it was time he thanked the Lord for the blessings he had instead of longing for something that could never be his.

The meal was quite pleasant, and once they'd finished, Natalie ran off to help Millie in the kitchen while he and Abigail went into the parlor.

&

Abigail breathed a sigh of relief. The family supper she'd planned had worked out well, and Nate seemed quite relaxed and at ease tonight. With Natalie in the kitchen with Millie, she might not have a better chance to broach the subject dearest to her heart.

She sat down on the settee and poured coffee from the pot her housekeeper had set on the table beside her. She put just a dollop of cream and two teaspoons of sugar in the cup, just as she knew Nate liked his after-dinner coffee, and handed it to him.

"Thank you, Abigail. Supper was delicious. And it was nice and peaceful."

"Did you have a bad day today, Nate? You seemed a bit dispirited when you arrived."

"It has been a busy week. Perhaps I'm just tired. I do appreciate that you weren't throwing a dinner party tonight.

I enjoyed the quiet evening."

Maybe she'd been going about things all wrong, Abigail thought. It had never occurred to her that he would enjoy a quiet, family-type meal more than one in the company of others. Maybe he was just now beginning to appreciate that kind of thing. Whatever it was, he seemed quite at ease with her, and she was going to take advantage of his mood.

"You know, Nate, I think you are just lonely. I think you miss being married. You need a wife as much as Natalie needs a mother."

For once, Nate didn't argue with her. "I've been thinking about that."

Abigail caught her breath. For a moment she was afraid she'd heard wrong and was afraid to speak. "That's good. That you've been giving it some thought."

He nodded and took a sip from his cup.

The thought that he might have someone—that Snow woman—in mind had her asking point-blank, "And is there someone you—"

"No." It came out rough and firm and told her more than she wanted to know.

He was hurting. Something had happened, but she wasn't going to ask about it. Instead, she was going to fight for what she wanted. She rose from the settee and went to sit on the footstool at Nate's feet. She looked him in the eyes and spoke from her heart. "You know, Nate, you will never find anyone who cares about you and Natalie the way I do. I've loved you both for a very long time."

"Abigail—"

"Please hear me out, Nate. Think about Rose. Can you think of anyone she would rather you marry than someone who loves you and Natalie as much as she did?" She didn't wait for his answer but continued, afraid he'd stop her at any moment. "It's what she would want, Nate. I know that you don't love me the way I love you. . .but I will try to make you happy."

There. She'd done it. She'd laid her heart at his feet.

Nate stood and pulled her to her feet. "You deserve more—"

"No." She shook her head. She had no time to lose. "Nate, think of Mama and Papa. They were devastated when Rose died. If you were to marry someone outside the family, they might lose some of the closeness they have with Natalie and you. And. . .well, married to me, you would never have to worry about your position at the bank. Think about it, Nate, dear. The best thing you could do for all of us is to marry me."

She held her breath, waiting to hear what he had to say, but Natalie burst into the room just then. "Papa, Aunt Abby! The cookies are nearly done. I can't wait to taste them!"

Abigail had never been more relieved in her life. At least she'd been saved from an outright refusal. "I can't wait, either, Natalie, dear."

"Neither can I. Should we go to the kitchen and grab one hot out of the oven?"

"Oh, let's!" Natalie said.

Abigail laid a hand on Nate's arm as they headed out of the room. "Just think about it, please."

Her heart leaped with joy as he nodded his head. He'd listened without getting angry and without telling her no. She could only hope that her plan to come between him and Miss Snow had worked. Now, maybe, just maybe, he'd come to his senses and see that he needed to keep his love and his daughter in his wife's family.

જ

For the next few days, Nate mulled over all Abigail had said. He'd been surprised when she dropped the conversation once

Natalie came to get them. It was as if she'd made her best case for marriage, and she was going to let him think about it.

Now as he left the bank and started walking home—it was too nice a day not to—he thought about it all over again. He'd been thinking about the past and the fire and how guilty he had felt that he hadn't been there when the fire reached his home, that he hadn't been able to save his wife. If only he'd gotten word about the fire earlier! But all the *if onlys* in the world could not change the events of that day, and he had accepted that long ago.

Still, he'd always wished for a different outcome. There was no way to get around the fact that, without Abigail, most likely Natalie would have died in the fire that day, too. A shiver went down his spine at the very thought. He would be forever grateful that Abigail had gotten his daughter to safety. He thought back over the last few years, back to the first few weeks when he'd been numb with pain. The whole family had been, but somehow they'd all managed to give Natalie the love and attention she needed, and no one gave her more attention than Abigail. There was also the fact that her father still thought Nate had gotten there in time to save Rose. Nate was sick of the guilt he felt that he couldn't save Jacob's youngest daughter. All Abigail had talked about had been true.

Normally, he would have brushed the conversation of the other night off and put it out of his mind until she brought it up again. But she'd been so right in many areas. Her parents would love nothing more than for Natalie to stay close, and the best way for that to happen would be if he and Abigail got married. This was also the first time she'd mentioned his needs, that he was lonely and needed a wife as much as Natalie needed a mother. The fact that the only woman he'd ever come to love besides Rose didn't seem to want to have anything to do with him. . .well, that most likely did play a part in his thinking these days, too.

If he thought for one moment that he had a chance with Meagan Snow, he would not even be giving the conversation with Abigail a second thought. But much to his disappointment, Meagan had made it quite clear that she wasn't interested in his courting her at all.

Natalie needed a mother, and he needed a wife. Abigail was quite right about all of that. She was also right about the fact that he didn't love her. . .not like she loved him. He wasn't sure he ever could. She seemed to understand that and still wanted them to marry. Could she be happy in a marriage to him under those circumstances? There was only one way to find out. She was having a dinner party the next night. He'd be the last one to leave for a change, and he would ask her.

❧

Once Nate told Abigail that he wanted to talk to her after everyone left, he began to have second thoughts. She had a look of expectancy about her, and he wasn't sure he was doing the right thing. But it was too late to change his mind now.

Abigail obviously wanted to know what he had to say, because she made sure no one lingered very long after dinner. As soon as the last couple took their leave, she led Nate into her parlor where she'd instructed her housekeeper to bring in coffee and the tea cakes she knew he was fond of.

"What is it you want to talk to me about, Nate?" She fixed his coffee for him and handed it to him along with one of the small cakes.

"I suppose it is about our conversation the other night."

Her cup rattled in its saucer before she steadied it. "Oh?"

"Yes. I've been giving everything you said some thought. I would like to remarry one day. It would be good to have someone to talk over the day with, to come home to at night."

Abigail kept silent, which surprised him. She nodded and took a sip of her coffee.

"And you are right about Natalie. She does want a mother. She would like me to marry again."

"I thought she would," Abigail said. She set her coffee down and clasped her hands together in her lap. "What else have you decided?"

Nate took a deep breath. "It will require both of us to make this decision."

She sat up straighter, and he knew he had her complete attention. "And what is that?"

"First—you said you know that I don't lo—"

"Love me like I love you?"

"Yes."

"I do know that."

"And you are willing to marry me anyway?"

Abigail joined him on the settee and took his hands in hers. "I am. Nate, I believe you will learn to love me."

At that moment, Nate truly hoped he could as he looked into her eyes. "In that case, then, will you marry me?"

Abigail leaned her head to one side and looked at him. Then her lips turned up in a smile. "Yes, Nate, I will marry you."

eighteen

Meagan's heart continued to break a little more each day after she turned down Nate's invitation to lunch. At church, she couldn't help but notice that Nate had stopped looking in her direction since she'd turned him down twice. She told herself it was best that way, but her heart told her differently.

While Nate wasn't looking for her, Abigail seemed intent on catching her eye and then pulling Nate a little closer as she placed a possessive hand through the crook of his arm. Her look seemed to say, *I told you so.*

Natalie always waved, but she didn't look as happy as she had just a few weeks ago, and Meagan's heart went out to her.

It came as no surprise when Abigail came into the shop the next day to pick up the last outfit Meagan had made for her to find that Nate was indeed getting married to her. "I want you to make my wedding dress, Miss Snow." She seemed to stress the *Miss* while she continued, "What plates do you have that I can choose from? But then, I've heard you are quite the designer. Do you think you could come up with a design for me?"

For a moment, Meagan was speechless. *Make this woman's wedding gown for her marriage to Nate?* If a knife had pierced her heart and been given a twist, she did not think it could give her any more pain than she felt at that moment. "I don't think I'm the one to make your wedding gown, Miss Connors. That is something I've never made before and—"

"Oh, nonsense! You do work comparable to some of my friends' gowns from Paris. There is no reason for you not to make my wedding gown unless. . ."

She paused, and Meagan held her breath. This woman was being much too nice.

"Unless you are hoping that Nate will change his mind and marry *you* instead of me?" Abigail continued.

She got right to the point, and she was exactly right. Meagan had wanted the first wedding gown she made to be her own. She'd been dreaming of walking down the aisle toward Nate for months. . .even after she knew it was hopeless.

"Miss Snow? Is that your problem? I do hope not. I want you to make this gown. And I'm sure my papa would not be pleased if you turn me down."

Turning her down was the very thing Meagan wanted to do. She'd never wanted to tell anyone to get out of her shop and never come back as badly as she did right at this moment. Abigail, however, was right. Her papa wouldn't be happy, and since Meagan still owed the bank on her loan, she couldn't risk making him angry. She'd already lost any chance for a life with Nate. She couldn't risk losing her family's livelihood.

"All right, Miss Connors. I'll make your gown."

"Good. That is what I was hoping to hear. I've set a wedding date for the seventeenth of July."

"That's very soon." It was June now, but Meagan told herself the sooner Nate was married, the sooner she could put him out of her mind. And the sooner she could finish Abigail's dress, the better. Perhaps once the woman had what she wanted, she would find another dressmaker to suit her needs. "But I will not design it. I won't have time. You'll have to choose from the plates I have."

Abigail made an irritated sound but didn't argue. "Very well, let's look at what you have."

Meagan pulled out several magazines for her to look at.

After poring over the different plates for the better part of the afternoon, Abigail finally decided on a lovely gown made of ivory satin draped with Brussels lace. Meagan was thankful that it wasn't anything like the gown she had pictured as her own. Abigail's choice was intricate, but Meagan had no doubt that she could make it.

Since she had no other appointments that day, they took careful measurements and found that there would need to be no changes from the last dress. That would make Meagan's job much easier, and for that she was extremely thankful.

By the time Abigail left the shop, Meagan was totally worn down. She was fully aware that the only way she'd been able to manage to act as if she wasn't heartbroken that Nate was marrying that woman was with the Lord's help. She prayed He'd be with her during the next month, giving her the strength she needed just to get through each day as she worked on the bridal gown for Abigail.

&

Even though Meagan prayed each night for strength to get through this trying time, it was all she could do to get through each day. Word of the upcoming marriage between Nate and Abigail had spread all over town.

She was worried about Natalie. At one time, the little girl had seemed so excited that her papa might marry again, but Meagan's mother told her she'd run into Natalie and her grandmother in town and asked if she was excited about all the wedding preparations and she had just shrugged. "She didn't look very happy to me," Meagan's mother had said.

And she didn't. At church, she looked sad, Nate looked resigned, and Meagan wasn't sure that even Abigail looked all that happy. Yet she had what she'd evidently always wanted. Hard as it was, Meagan began praying that Nate and Natalie would be happy, although she couldn't bring herself to add Abigail to that prayer, not yet—and she wasn't sure she'd ever be able to.

When Abigail and her mother brought Natalie in to ask if Meagan would make her dress, also, there was no way Meagan could turn them down. It was wonderful to see Natalie again, and she seemed happy to see Meagan. Still, there was a sadness in her eyes that Meagan didn't like. She wished she could ask Natalie what was wrong, but with Abigail and her mother within hearing distance, there was no way to do it. All she really could do was pray that the little girl would be happy with the new developments in her life. The one bright light in all of it seemed to be that she got to see Natalie again.

With all the heartache involved in making clothes for the wedding of the man she loved, taking care to make Abigail's dress come up to the high standards she'd set for herself when she went into business was one of the hardest things Meagan had ever done. But her reputation and her family's livelihood depended on her. She didn't for one moment think that Nate would let the bank foreclose on her, but Abigail could make sure no one would want to come to her shop if she wasn't satisfied with her dress.

So Meagan stayed up late, working to make sure that the trim was just so, that the lace draped perfectly on the mannequin she'd padded out to match Abigail's measurements. She did take part of Independence Day off to watch the parade and have a picnic at Basin Park with her family; then it was back to work as soon as they got back home. Sarah had shown a great interest in learning to sew and helping Meagan in the shop, and Meagan was grateful. She could use all the help she could get.

When Abigail insisted that Meagan come to Nate's house

for her and Natalie's last fittings a week before the wedding, she agreed only because Nate would be at work. Abigail seemed intent on rubbing salt into the wounds she'd already inflicted. But the thought of being alone with Abigail at Nate's home was just too intimidating, so Meagan took Sarah along for support.

Nate's housekeeper, Mrs. Baker, showed Meagan and Sarah up the stairs and to Natalie's room. Nate's home was beautiful, and Meagan wondered if Abigail would move in after their wedding or if Nate and Natalie would live in her home. Somehow, she couldn't think that Abigail's home would be as warm and inviting as Nate's. His housekeeper had a knack for making it feel homey, and then there was the fact that Natalie lived there.

"Miss Meg, I've been waiting for you to get here," Natalie said when Meagan entered the child's room. "I wanted to run down and greet you, but Aunt Abby said no." The look the little girl gave her aunt spoke volumes to Meagan. Natalie was not happy with her aunt at all.

"She's here now, Natalie. I told you to quit whining, and she'd be here soon."

Tears welled in Natalie's eyes, but she answered Meagan's smile with one of her own.

"Sarah, would you please help Miss Connors try on her dress while I get Natalie's on her?"

"Natalie can wait—"

"There's no need for that. I brought my sister to help me out today."

"Very well." Abigail's tone was unusually sweet. "She can help Natalie while you help me."

Meagan nodded at her sister. There was no point in irritating Abigail more than she already seemed to be.

Meagan would have preferred to be helping Natalie. But as they were all in the same room, there was no way to have a private conversation with her and ask how she was doing. She could only hope the little girl knew how much she cared that she was upset.

Abigail stood in front of the corner mirror while Meagan helped her off with her wrapper and on with the bustle she'd need for the wedding dress. Then she stood on a stool to raise the dress over Abigail's head and down over her corset, chemise, petticoats, and bustle. It was going to look wonderful on her. Meagan could tell as she buttoned the tiny buttons up the back and settled the skirts around her. It fit her to perfection, and hard as it was to say, she told the truth. "It looks beautiful on you, Miss Connors."

Abigail turned this way and that in front of the mirror. The train was just the right length, and the veil framed her face perfectly. "I do look wonderful, don't I, Natalie, dear?"

Natalie ran over to her aunt. "It's very pretty, Aunt Abby. May I see how my dress looks?"

"In a moment, Natalie." Abigail twisted and turned once more before moving out of the way.

"I'll help you out of the dress, Miss Connors," Sarah said. "My sister needs to check the hem on Natalie's dress."

"Why it looks perfectly straight to me," Abigail said, but she let Sarah help her out of the dress while Natalie preened in front of the mirror.

"Oh, it's beautiful, Miss Meg! I love it," the young girl said. The dress was of satin and lace but was a soft buttery yellow, fitting for a young girl.

"Thank you, Natalie. I'm glad you like it. It fits you perfectly, and you look beautiful in it. I just need to make sure the hem is right." Meagan had her make slow turns until she was certain the hem was level. "It is just right."

"You need to take if off if Miss Snow is through inspecting it. You don't want to get it dirty, Natalie."

"I won't get it dirty, Aunt Abby."

"Natalie, take it off, now."

Meagan wasn't sure who she was trying to impress by her tone, but it certainly wasn't her. She didn't like the way Abigail was speaking to her niece.

"Do I have to?"

"Natalie! I can't believe your impertinence! Now go change!"

Meagan held her breath and glanced at her sister. How dare the woman speak to Natalie like that? She was just a child excited about a new dress.

Natalie turned to do as she was told, but then she began to cry. "I wish my daddy never said he would marry you, Aunt Abby! I wanted him to marry Miss Meg—not you!"

Abigail grabbed her arm. "I'll not have that attitude, either. You—"

Natalie pulled her arm away and ran for the bedroom door. She ran out of the room, yelling, "I don't want you to be my mama!"

Meagan followed her first instinct to run after the little girl, but she wasn't fast enough. A scream she knew she would never forget sent chills down her spine as she reached the landing. At the bottom of the stairs lay Natalie.

nineteen

Meagan went into action as soon as she reached the bottom of the stairs. Natalie was breathing, but she wasn't responding. Her arm seemed bent at an odd angle, and Meagan was afraid to move her. As Abigail seemed incapable of helping her, Meagan hurriedly sent her sister for Nate and asked the housekeeper to get the doctor.

Abigail began sobbing and couldn't seem to stop. It seemed forever before Nate burst through the door. He arrived out of breath and with fear in his eyes. Bending over his daughter, he took one look at Abigail and then looked to Meagan to tell them what happened.

"It was an accident. She got upset and ran out of the room, and then we heard a yell and. . ." Meagan prayed for the Lord to keep her tears at bay. She had a feeling Nate couldn't take that right now. "When I got to the landing, she was at the bottom of the stairs." Her heart twisted just seeing the pain in Nate's eyes.

The doctor arrived and quickly checked for broken bones. He tried to rouse Natalie once more to no avail. Afraid to jostle her into a carriage or wagon for the trip to the doctor's home, he had the child transferred to her bedroom. Abigail managed to go up to turn down the bed, but Meagan thought she was suffering from shock.

Meagan knew she would never forget the look on Nate's face when he gently picked up his limp daughter and carried her upstairs. It was only then, as she stayed behind for a few minutes to pray, that she let the tears flow.

She sent Sarah to tell Abigail's parents and their mother. "Let Mama know I might be here awhile. I think Abigail is in shock and I...I just can't leave right now."

Sarah gave her a hug. "I will. We'll be back to check on you all."

Meagan nodded and hugged her back. Then she gave her a little push. She rushed up the stairs. This wasn't her family and maybe it wasn't her place to stay, but she had to find out how Natalie was and see if Nate or Abigail needed anything.

When Meagan stopped just inside the bedroom door, she saw the doctor bent over Natalie. Nate and Abigail stood at the foot of the bed. Meagan waited to hear what the doctor had to say.

He turned to Nate. "Her left arm is broken, and I'll need to set it. But I'm more concerned that she's not responsive. Most likely, she is suffering from a concussion. We'll have to watch her closely. I'd prefer to have her in my office, but I don't want to move her right now." He looked at Abigail and then over at Meagan. "Would you get Nate's housekeeper? I'm going to need her help setting the bone."

Meagan nodded and turned to find the housekeeper right behind her. "The doctor needs your help."

Mrs. Baker nodded and hurried to the doctor's side. "What do you need me to do?"

"Get some water for the plaster and help me set her arm. Do you think you can do that?"

"Of course. I'll be right back with the water." She took one look at Natalie, shook her head, and hurried out of the room.

Meagan was right behind her. "Can I help?"

Nate's housekeeper was on her way to gather a pail of

warm water from the stove's reservoir, along with several rags. She shook her head. "Just pray. Poor baby. I just hope she won't be feeling the pain of having that arm set."

A shiver shot right through Meagan at the very thought that Natalie was suffering, and she sent up a silent prayer that the child would be all right.

Meagan followed the housekeeper out of the kitchen, and when the door knocker sounded, Mrs. Baker turned to her. "I'm sure that's Mr. and Mrs. Connors. Will you show them upstairs?"

"Of course I will." Meagan hurried to answer the door, and it was Mr. and Mrs. Connors. Sarah had filled them in on the accident, and Meagan led them up even though they knew the way. They looked so worried, she didn't want to send them up by themselves. She could see that Nate was standing at the end of his daughter's bed and Abigail was just staring into space when her parents arrived. Meagan's heart went out to her. She knew it had been an accident, but she had a feeling Abigail would be blaming herself.

The housekeeper was bustling around getting things ready for the doctor when he turned and said, "All right, everyone. It's time to leave the room until we get this arm set. Then you can come back in."

"Doc, I don't want to leave. I can help."

"I know you don't want to leave, Nate. But it would be hard on you to stay, and it will make my job quicker and much easier if you go. I'll let you back in as soon as I'm done."

Abigail's mother took her arm and led her into the hallway. Her father put a hand to Nate's shoulder. Nate simply nodded and turned to leave the room. Meagan stood slightly away from them all but couldn't bring herself to go downstairs.

Nate moved to the staircase and looked down. What must

be going through his mind? Meagan couldn't keep herself from going to him. "You know that we're all praying she comes through this."

He looked down at her. "I know you are. I. . .thank you for being here and for sending for me."

"You are welcome. I—" Meagan broke off, unable to continue. Just the look in Nate's eyes had tears welling in hers. *He's lost a wife, dear Lord. Please don't let him lose his daughter, too.* She didn't know what else to say or do.

"Is there any tea made, do you know?" Mrs. Connors asked.

Relieved to have something to do, Meagan said, "I'll go make some tea and bring it up, if that is all right?"

Nate didn't seem to hear her, and Abigail only stared at her. Mrs. Connors nodded and said, "That would be very helpful. Thank you, Miss Snow."

Meagan hurried back to the kitchen and put water on for the tea. While it was heating, she readied a tea tray with cream and sugar, cups, and saucers. She prayed while the tea was steeping. "Dear Lord, please let Natalie be all right. I don't know what it would do to this family if they lost her. And I—my whole family has come to love her, too, Lord. And You know how I feel about Nate. Please keep him from any more heartache. Please let Natalie heal and come back to us. In Jesus' name I pray. Amen."

She turned and gave a start to see Nate standing there looking at her.

"Meagan. . .I. . .thank you for that prayer. I—" He stopped and sighed. "I couldn't stand there just waiting for Doc to let me back in. Let me carry the tray up for you."

"All right." She handed it to him. She didn't know whether to go or stay until he looked back.

"You're coming, too, aren't you?"

"Of course." There was no way she could let this family go through this alone. She followed Nate up the staircase.

๙

The doctor was just coming out of the room when Nate and Meagan got to the landing. Nate quickly set the tray on a table outside Natalie's door. "How is she?"

"She's still unconscious. But her arm is set, and she's breathing normally. I believe she will come out of this, Nate. I've seen cases similar to this too many times not to believe she'll be all right. I'll check in later."

Nate knew there was no guarantee, but suddenly he felt hope. "Thank you. I pray you are right. I'll see you out."

"No. I can see myself out. You stay with your daughter."

For the first time since Nate got there, Abigail spoke. "Miss Snow can go with you. She's not needed anymore."

"Abigail!" Mrs. Connors protested. "Miss Snow's presence has been comforting. And she's made some tea which will taste mighty good to me right now." She turned and looked at Meagan. "I'm sorry about my daughter's rudeness. She's just upset about Natalie."

"That's understandable," Meagan said. "I can go home. My mother and I will check and see if you all need anything a little later."

"No." Nate put out a hand to stop her. He wanted her here beside him. . .just in case. "I don't want you to go. Natalie will want to see you when she wakes up."

Abigail shrugged before following him back into the room. Nate pulled a chair close to Natalie's bed and took hold of her hand. She looked so small and defenseless lying there. He heard Meagan say, "I'll get Mrs. Connors some tea. Would you like a cup, Miss Connors?"

Abigail was silent.

"Nate?"

"Not just yet, thank you." It gave him comfort to hear her voice in the room.

"I'll take a cup," Abigail's father said.

Nate glanced over at his in-laws and could see the pain in their eyes. They'd lost their youngest daughter and now there was the possibility—no! He couldn't think that way, wouldn't think that way.

His glance slid to Abigail. She was just staring into space. She seemed near collapse. Anyone could look at her and see that.

Meagan took the tea to Mr. and Mrs. Connors, and Nate heard them whisper their thanks. The wait was grueling. Nate bowed his head and whispered, "Dear Lord, please be with my Natalie. I can't lose her, Lord. Please heal her and bring her back to me. You said You won't give us more than we can handle, and Lord, I don't think I could stand it if—please, Lord, I beg You to let my baby be all right."

Suddenly he heard the crash of a teacup, and then Georgette exclaimed, "Nate! Natalie's eyes are blinking!"

His head came up, and he looked closely at his daughter. Everyone else in the room gathered around the bed, looking at Natalie. . .even Meagan. There was a flutter, and then another. The little girl's eyes slowly opened and then shut. Opened and shut again. . .and then opened. "Papa?"

"I'm—" Nate's voice broke. "I'm here, my precious girl."

"My arm hurts, Papa."

"I know. You fell—"

"Down the stairs. I was running away from Aunt Abby and I fell. . .just like Mama did."

Nate caught his breath. This was the first time Natalie had ever mentioned her mother or the fall. "But you are going to be all right, Natalie, dear. You have a broken arm, and once it heals, you'll be fine."

Natalie didn't seem to hear him. Instead, she was looking at Abigail. "I fell, Aunt Abby. Just like Mama did. And it was all your fault!"

"No!" Abigail screamed. "It was *not* my fault. I was trying to keep Rose from going back upstairs for her precious mementos!" She began to cry deep, wrenching sobs. "I was trying to get us all out of there. But. . .but. . ." She sobbed again. "When I grabbed her, she tried to pull away from me and lost her balance. Then she. . .I. . ." Her voice trickled away.

"Abigail, dear, we know you didn't mean to. . . ." Her mother put an arm around her, but Abigail pulled away.

"I don't want you to marry Aunt Abigail, Papa!" Natalie was crying now. "I want you to marry Miss Meg!"

"Oh, Natalie. I'm so sorry. I'm an awful person. I've made Nate feel guilty for not being there to save her. All the time I resented that he loved Rose and not me! And then. . .I made Miss Snow think that he was. . .in love with me so that she wouldn't give him the time of day—so that he would finally realize it was me he needed to marry. But he loves her! I'm sorry. I'm so sorry!" She yanked the engagement ring Nate had given her off her finger and forced it into his hand, tears flowing down her face. Then she turned and ran out of the room.

Holding the ring he'd given Abigail, Nate felt an over-whelming sense of relief that she'd broken the engagement, but he was speechless as he watched her run out of the room. He knew that Abigail could be manipulative, but to go to such lengths to get her way? And to purposefully add to the guilt he'd felt that he couldn't save Rose? It was hard to take it all in. But what pained him most was that she'd set out to ruin his relationship with Meagan so that he would ask her to marry him. Anger deep and hot rose up, and all he could do was look at Meagan. The color was high on her cheeks, and she looked as shocked as he felt.

"Abigail!" Mrs. Connors looked totally taken aback at her daughter's words. She didn't seem to know what to do.

"I'll go after her. She's in no shape to be by herself," Jacob Connors said. He crossed the room to kiss Natalie. "I love you, and I'll be back in a little while, all right?"

Natalie nodded. "Yes, Grandfather."

Georgette hurried over to the bed and gave her grand-daughter a kiss on the cheek. "Natalie, dear, God has answered our prayers that you will be all right. We love you so very much. And your aunt Abigail loves you with all her heart." Georgette wiped the tears streaming from her eyes. "She never meant to harm anyone. I—Nate, I must go with Jacob and Abigail. We need to get her home. She's not—"

He nodded. Abigail was in no condition to be alone, but he wasn't the one who could help her. He needed to stay with his daughter and Meagan. "She needs you. Go to her. Natalie knows you'll be back soon."

It was quiet in the room once the Connors family left. Nate wasn't sure what to say, and Meagan didn't seem to know what to do as she stood beside Natalie's bed, wiping tears from her own eyes. But when she finally looked at him, Nate began to hope.

twenty

Meagan's heart was thumping so hard she could barely breathe, seeing the look in Nate's eyes. He approached her slowly, his lips turning up in a slight smile. She couldn't take her gaze from his.

"Was Abigail right? Did she make you think I was in love with her?"

Meagan bit her bottom lip and nodded but couldn't find her voice.

"It all makes sense now. You must have thought me quite the cad when I kept asking you to have dinner and then lunch with me." He lifted her face to his. "I'm sorry. I certainly helped her cause when I asked her to marry me, didn't I?"

"I didn't know what to think. I. . .didn't think you were the kind of person who would act that way, yet everything Abigail was saying to me when she came into the shop told me something completely different from what I thought was happening between us."

Nate shook his head and looked deep into her eyes. "I can see how you would be confused and not want to have anything to do with me. But when you kept refusing to see me, I thought you didn't care."

"Oh, Nate." Meagan shook her head. "I'm sorry, I—"

"It isn't your fault, Meagan. But I knew I would never find anyone like you again. And if you didn't want me, as I thought, well, I hoped I could one day come to love Abigail. Natalie needs a mother, and. . .I thought I was doing the right thing. I didn't treat her right, either. I was just so. . . heartbroken. I had no hope that you would ever return my feelings, and—"

"Oh, Nate, I don't know what to say. I did—I do care about you very much. I just didn't know what to think, and then once you were engaged, there was nothing more to do."

Nate bent his head and whispered in her ear, "You are the woman I want to marry. I love you, Meagan Snow. I've loved you for quite a while now, and I wish I'd told you long ago. I love you with all my heart. Do you think you can give me another chance to win yours?"

Meagan pulled back just enough to look him in the eye. "My heart is already yours. You won it a long time ago. I love you, too, Nate."

His lips claimed hers softly at first until Meagan returned the pressure, and then he deepened the kiss. Meagan's eyes filled with tears. Nate loved her. Not Abigail—but her. Her world righted itself for the first time in weeks.

She broke the kiss and looked into Nate's eyes. She could see the joy she felt reflected in his eyes.

"Will you marry me, Meagan? Will you take my heart as your own and be my wife and Natalie's mother?"

"I love you, Nate. I will be honored to become your wife and the mother of your daughter, whom I love, also."

His lips found hers once more in a kiss meant to assure her of just how much he loved her. Time forgotten, they were broken apart by the child they both loved yelling, "Yippee! We're going to marry Miss Meg!"

Nate chuckled and looked a little embarrassed. Apparently Meagan wasn't the only one who'd forgotten that Natalie was in the same room and overheard everything they said.

When they hurried over to Natalie and included her in

a hug, Meagan was more than a little aware that if Natalie hadn't taken that fall, she and Nate might never have known how the other felt. She thanked the Lord once again that Natalie was going to be all right. How doubly blessed they were this evening.

❧

The doctor arrived at the same time Meagan's mother and sisters did. They were all in the room while the doctor looked into Natalie's eyes and checked her cast before pronouncing her on the mend. He recommended a light supper if she was hungry but told Nate not to worry if her appetite wasn't up to par. He gave her some medicine that would ease her pain and help her sleep during the night, should she need it.

"It does my heart good to see you awake, child," he said to Natalie. "You look quite chipper for someone who broke an arm and had a concussion to go along with it."

Natalie's smile was huge when she nodded. "I'm very happy!"

"I'm sure you are no happier than your papa and these good folk here with him."

"Can I tell them, Papa?" Natalie giggled excitedly.

Nate grinned and pulled Meagan into the crook of his arm. "Go right ahead."

Meagan's mother and sisters looked at her curiously. She just smiled back.

"Tell us what, Natalie, dear?" Mrs. Snow asked.

"Papa and Miss Meg are going to get married! She's going to be my new mama! And I will be part of your family!"

"You are? How wonderful for us!" Meagan's mother seemed truly confused when she looked at Natalie. "But what? How?"

"It all happened 'cause of my fall," Natalie said. "Aunt Abby gave Papa his ring back, and then after she left, Papa and

Miss Meg said they love each other, and I saw them kissing!"

Meagan couldn't contain her joy any longer. "Nate asked me to marry him, Mama. And I told him yes."

"Oh, my dears. That is wonderful news. But what about—"

"We'll tell you later," Meagan said.

Her mother nodded, and Meagan knew she understood that there was quite a bit left unsaid.

"My, we do have much to celebrate!"

It was a while later before Meagan and Nate could discuss wedding plans. By the time her family had left, with Nate promising to bring her home once Natalie was asleep and his housekeeper could watch her, Meagan had begun to believe it was all true and not part of her dreams.

After a light supper, Meagan had helped Natalie get ready for bed, and the child was so sweet even with her pain, that she knew Natalie truly loved her. It felt very natural to kiss the child good night and wait for Nate to do the same. They didn't go far in case she called out. Instead of going downstairs, they took a seat on a settee in the wide hallway. There was so much to talk about as she told him how Abigail had gone about convincing her that Nate and she were going to be married.

"I can't help but feel sorry for her," Meagan said.

"I know. I never realized how guilty she felt about Rose's death. I was too busy blaming myself for not getting there in time, I suppose. I should never have asked her to marry me when I didn't love her like I do you."

"You need to talk to her, Nate. She's devastated that Natalie is upset with her. I saw her face when Natalie told her she wanted you to marry me."

Nate rubbed a hand over his face and shook his head. "I still can't believe this day. I was so afraid I was going to lose my daughter and to end it with her all right and knowing I have you. . .I have so much to thank the Lord for!" He bent his head and captured her lips with his own.

Meagan wondered if there would ever be a sweeter kiss between them. But when he raised his head for only a second and then kissed her again, she knew there could be.

"When are you going to become my wife? I don't want to wait long. I don't want to take a chance on anything going wrong again."

She kissed his cheek. "Nothing is going to go wrong—not now. We'll get married as soon as I can get my wedding gown made and you can talk to Abigail and let her know that she will always be part of Natalie's life. I would never want Rose's family to think that they couldn't come around or be as much a part of her life as they always have been. Please, Nate, let them know."

Nate cupped his hand around her chin and looked down at her. If she'd ever doubted his love for her, she no longer did. It was shining from his eyes.

"I'll let them know," he promised. . .just before he kissed her, telling her in his own way just how very much he loved her.

 За

Nate didn't see Abigail or her parents for the next several days, but Jacob and Georgette came to see Natalie often, bringing her a toy or some other treat. He'd talked to them briefly, but he didn't feel any animosity from them about the broken engagement to Abigail. Georgette stayed most of the day while Nate was at work, but she usually left just before he got home, and he hadn't been able to really talk to them about their daughter. Abigail hadn't come to see Natalie at all. Natalie didn't seem too concerned about it. Nate tried to tell her that her aunt Abigail loved her, but Natalie didn't want to talk about it just yet.

By the end of the week, Nate was determined to keep his promise to Meagan. He left work on Friday and went to Abigail's home. She did need reassurance that Natalie still loved her, and he'd promised to let her know that she would be a part of Natalie's life always. But Abigail wasn't at her home, or at least that's what her housekeeper told him. Nate sought her out at her parents' home. He was shown into the study where Mr. Connors seemed to be waiting for him.

"Good evening, Nate. Please, take a seat. I suppose you've come to talk about my daughter."

"I've come to see her, sir."

"She's had a hard time. I had no idea she blamed herself for so much." Jacob sighed deeply.

Nate nodded. "I. . .know. Neither did I. I want to assure her that Natalie will come around. I know she didn't mean to make Rose fall down the stairs that day. And I should have told you earlier that as much as I wanted to save Rose, I didn't get there in time. The house was engulfed in flames when I got there."

"I know that, son."

"You do?"

"I know most people in this town, Nate. They tell me things. But I also know how much you loved Rose. I know you would have gone in there and dragged her out if there were any way you could have."

Nate blinked against the tears that threatened. "I would have."

Jacob nodded. "Abigail isn't the woman for you. I know it, and you know it. You never had to marry her to stay part of this family, Nate."

"Thank you, sir. I am sorry I hurt Abigail. I prayed that

I was doing the right thing when I asked her to marry me. What I should have done was pray for the Lord to guide me in doing the right thing. I didn't wait on Him. It would have been easier on Abigail if I'd done that."

"One day, she'll get what she needs. A love all her own—not one that loved her sister first or who is in love with someone else, but one who loves her."

"I'll pray she does. I would like to apologize to her. Do you think she'll talk to me?"

"Not now, Nate. She doesn't want to talk to anyone—not even her friends."

Nate sighed, whether from frustration or relief he didn't know, but at least he could tell Meagan that he had tried. "I understand. I—"

"I'll tell her you came by, Nate. She'll be all right. We're going to see to it that she is."

Nate couldn't help but wonder whom Jacob was trying to convince. . .Nate or himself.

"I like Miss Snow." Jacob changed the subject, taking Nate by surprise. "Natalie told us about you asking her to marry you. We'll be invited to the wedding?"

"Oh yes, you will. Meagan wanted me to assure Abigail, and you and Georgette, that she wants you all to be as much a part of Natalie's life as you always have been. She knows how deeply you love Natalie."

"That does my heart good to hear, Nate. Let her know she'll be part of ours, too. I think Rose would have liked her."

Nate left the Connors' home feeling blessed, indeed. Blessed that Natalie was all right, blessed that Jacob and Georgette would continue to be part of his life, and blessed to be in love with a woman who wanted it no other way.

epilogue

September 3, 1886

Meagan's wedding day dawned bright and sunny. She'd finished her dress only two days before, but it was just as she'd imagined it. She'd made it as different from Abigail's as she possibly could. It was of white satin and lace, but it was much simpler than Abigail's, and she loved it.

Now as she waited to walk down the aisle toward her husband-to-be, Meagan felt completely blessed. Nate was the most wonderful man in the world. When she'd expressed a worry about her mother and sisters, he'd taken her in his arms.

"Meagan, my love, don't you know that I would never let them suffer because of our marriage? My home is large enough for you all. However, what I thought I might do is pay off your loan and give the title to your home back to your mother free and clear. She and the girls could continue to live in the home they love if that is what they wish."

"But I don't want her to have to work—I mean I love the shop and. . .I don't—"

"Meagan. Your mother will never have to work outside the home again. And you have a talent. If you want to continue with the business you've worked so hard to get started, that is fine with me. I would hope that you wouldn't feel you must work night and day, though. I'd like to spend time with you. Perhaps you could continue to teach Sarah to sew, if she's interested, and she could help out. Then she would have a career until she finds some nice young man whom we approve of."

He did care about her family, and he'd been thinking about their future just as she had. Having answered all her worries, Meagan had reached up and pulled his dear face down to hers so that she could look him in the eye. "You are the dearest man in the world. Oh! How I love you."

Nate had taken advantage of their close proximity and claimed her lips in a kiss that more than convinced her he felt the same toward her. She had no complaints at all.

Now, as the wedding march began, she slowly followed Natalie down the aisle to Nate, who was standing at the front of the church. Her eyes on him, she barely noticed who was there to witness the happiest day of her life. She did see her family on one side of the aisle and Mr. and Mrs. Conners on the other side. She felt additionally blessed to see Rose's parents there to witness their vows. Those were the only people she was concerned with today—their loved ones witnessing her and Nate's vow to love and honor each other for the rest of their lives.

As the minister pronounced them man and wife, Meagan raised her face to Nate.

"I love you, my wife," he whispered just before his lips met hers. Meagan thanked the Lord above for all of her blessings and most especially that He had given her a love for keeps.

A Letter To Our Readers

Dear Reader:

In order that we might better contribute to your reading enjoyment, we would appreciate your taking a few minutes to respond to the following questions. We welcome your comments and read each form and letter we receive. When completed, please return to the following:

Fiction Editor
Heartsong Presents
PO Box 719
Uhrichsville, Ohio 44683

1. Did you enjoy reading *A Love For Keeps* by Janet Lee Barton?
   ❑ Very much! I would like to see more books by this author!
   ❑ Moderately. I would have enjoyed it more if

   _____

   _____

   _____

2. Are you a member of **Heartsong Presents**? ❑ Yes ❑ No
   If no, where did you purchase this book? _____

   _____

3. How would you rate, on a scale from 1 (poor) to 5 (superior), the cover design? _____

4. On a scale from 1 (poor) to 10 (superior), please rate the following elements.

   ____ Heroine   ____ Plot
   ____ Hero   ____ Inspirational theme
   ____ Setting   ____ Secondary characters

5. These characters were special because? _____
_____
_____

6. How has this book inspired your life? _____
_____
_____

7. What settings would you like to see covered in future
   Heartsong Presents books? _____
_____
_____

8. What are some inspirational themes you would like to see
   treated in future books? _____
_____
_____

9. Would you be interested in reading other **Heartsong
   Presents** titles? ❏ Yes ❏ No

10. Please check your age range:
    ❏ Under 18   ❏ 18-24
    ❏ 25-34   ❏ 35-45
    ❏ 46-55   ❏ Over 55

Name_____
Occupation _____
Address _____
City, State, Zip_____

DESERT ROSES

Dreaming of a fresh start and establishing their roots in a new place brings three women to the New Mexico Territory in the 1890s.

Will faith and love be the foundation for a new home near Farmington, or will the challenges of the Wild West send these women hurrying back to civilization?

Historical, paperback, 352 pages, 5³/₁₆" x 8"

Please send me _____ copies of *Desert Roses*. I am enclosing $7.97 for each.
(Please add $4.00 to cover postage and handling per order. OH add 7% tax.
If outside the U.S. please call 740-922-7280 for shipping charges.)

Name_____

Address _____

City, State, Zip _____

To place a credit card order, call 1-740-922-7280.
Send to: Heartsong Presents Readers' Service, PO Box 721, Uhrichsville, OH 44683

Heart♥ng

Any 12 Heartsong Presents titles for only $27.00*

HISTORICAL ROMANCE IS CHEAPER BY THE DOZEN!

Buy any assortment of twelve *Heartsong Presents* titles and save 25% off of the already discounted price of $2.97 each!

*plus $4.00 shipping and handling per order and sales tax where applicable.
If outside the U.S. please call
740-922-7280 for shipping charges.

HEARTSONG PRESENTS TITLES AVAILABLE NOW:

(If ordering from this page, please remember to include it with the order form.)

Presents

Great Inspirational Romance at a Great Price!

Heartsong Presents books are inspirational romances in
contemporary and historical settings, designed to give you an
enjoyable, spirit-lifting reading experience. You can choose
wonderfully written titles from some of today's best authors like
Wanda E. Brunstetter, Mary Connealy, Susan Page Davis,
Cathy Marie Hake, Joyce Livingston, and many others.

When ordering quantities less than twelve, above titles are $2.97 each.
Not all titles may be available at time of order.

HEARTSONG
PRESENTS

If you love Christian romance...

$10.⁹⁹

You'll love Heartsong Presents'
inspiring and faith-filled romances by
today's very best Christian authors...Wanda E. Brunstetter,
Mary Connealy, Susan Page Davis, Cathy Marie Hake, and
Joyce Livingston, to mention a few!

When you join Heartsong Presents, you'll enjoy four
brand-new, mass market, 176-page books—two contemporary
and two historical—that will build you up in your faith when
you discover God's role in every relationship you read about!

Mass Market 176 Pages

Imagine...four new romances every
four weeks—with men and women like you
who long to meet the one God has chosen as
the love of their lives...all for the low price
of $10.99 postpaid.

To join, simply visit www.heartsong
presents.com or complete the coupon
below and mail it to the address provided.

✂------------------------------

YES! Sign me up for Heartsong!

NEW MEMBERSHIPS WILL BE SHIPPED IMMEDIATELY!
Send no money now. We'll bill you only $10.99
postpaid with your first shipment of four books. Or for
faster action, call 1-740-922-7280.

NAME_____

ADDRESS_____

CITY_____ STATE _____ ZIP _____

MAIL TO: HEARTSONG PRESENTS, P.O. Box 721, Uhrichsville, Ohio 44683
or sign up at WWW.HEARTSONGPRESENTS.COM